PENGUIN BOOKS

MEMORIES OF MY MELANCHOLY WHORES

'A velvety pleasure to read . . . Márquez has composed,
with his usual sensual gravity and Olympian humour,
a love letter to the dying light'
John Updike

'There is not one stale sentence, redundant word or
unfinished thought'
The Times

'Márquez describes this amorous, sometimes disturbing journey
with the grace and vigour of a master storyteller'
Daily Mail

'Márquez is wonderful on the transformative and
redemptive powers of love. Storytelling magic'
Tatler

'The most important writer of fiction in any language'
Bill Clinton

'Profoundly haunting . . . one of literature's great figures pushes
back the years and gives us fiction of the very highest order'
The Times Literary Supplement

'Full of arresting meditations on love, nostalgia and mortality'
Daily Telegraph

MEMORIES OF
MY MELANCHOLY
WHORES

GABRIEL
GARCÍA
MÁRQUEZ

TRANSLATED FROM
THE SPANISH
BY EDITH GROSSMAN

PENGUIN BOOKS

PENGUIN BOOKS

Published by the Penguin Group
Penguin Books Ltd, 80 Strand, London WC2R 0RL, England
Penguin Group (USA), Inc., 375 Hudson Street, New York, New York 10014, USA
Penguin Group (Canada), 90 Eglinton Avenue East, Suite 700, Toronto, Ontario, Canada M4P 2Y3
(a division of Pearson Penguin Canada Inc.)
Penguin Ireland, 25 St Stephen's Green, Dublin 2, Ireland (a division of Penguin Books Ltd)
Penguin Group (Australia), 250 Camberwell Road, Camberwell, Victoria 3124, Australia
(a division of Pearson Australia Group Pty Ltd)
Penguin Books India Pvt Ltd, 11 Community Centre, Panchsheel Park, New Delhi – 110 017, India
Penguin Group (NZ), 67 Apollo Drive, Rosedale, North Shore 0632, New Zealand
(a division of Pearson New Zealand Ltd)
Penguin Books (South Africa) (Pty) Ltd, 24 Sturdee Avenue, Rosebank, Johannesburg 2196, South Africa

Penguin Books Ltd, Registered Offices: 80 Strand, London WC2R 0RL, England

www.penguin.com

Originally published in Spain as *Memoria de mis putas tristes* by Mondadori
(Grijalbo Mondadori, S. A.), Barcelona, and in hardcover in Spanish in the United States
by Alfred A. Knopf, a division of Random House, Inc., New York 2005
First published in Great Britain by Jonathan Cape 2005
Published in Penguin Books 2006
This edition published 2007
Copyright © 2005 by Gabriel García Márquez.
Copyright © 2005 by Mondadori (Grijalbo Mondadori, S. A.)

3

The moral right of the author has been asserted

Printed in England by Clays Ltd, St Ives plc

ISBN: 978-0-141-02873-6

www.greenpenguin.co.uk

Penguin Books is committed to a sustainable future
for our business, our readers and our planet.
The book in your hands is made from paper
certified by the Forest Stewardship Council.

"He was not to do anything in bad taste, the woman of the inn warned old Eguchi. He was not to put his finger into the mouth of the sleeping girl, or try anything else of that sort."

—YASUNARI KAWABATA,
House of the Sleeping Beauties

Memories of
My Melancholy Whores

1

THE YEAR I turned ninety, I wanted to give myself the gift of a night of wild love with an adolescent virgin. I thought of Rosa Cabarcas, the owner of an illicit house who would inform her good clients when she had a new girl available. I never succumbed to that or to any of her many other lewd temptations, but she did not believe in the purity of my principles. Morality, too, is a question of time, she would say with a malevolent smile, you'll see. She was a little younger than I, and I hadn't heard anything about her for so many years that she very well might have died. But after the first ring I recognized the voice on the phone, and with no preambles I fired at her:

"Today's the day."

She sighed: Ah, my sad scholar, you disappear for twenty years and come back only to ask for the impossible. She regained mastery of her art at once and offered me half a dozen delectable options, but all of them, to be frank, were used. I said no, insisting the girl had to be a virgin and available that very night. She asked in alarm: What are you trying to prove? Nothing, I replied, wounded to the core, I know very well what I can and cannot do. Unmoved, she said that scholars may know it all, but they don't know everything: The only Virgos left in the world are people like you who were born in August. Why didn't you give me more time? Inspiration gives no warnings, I said. But perhaps it can wait, she said, always more knowledgeable than any man, and she asked for just two days to make a thorough investigation of the market. I replied in all seriousness that in an affair such as this, at my age, each hour is like a year. Then it can't be done, she said without the slightest doubt, but it doesn't matter, it's more exciting this way, what the hell, I'll call you in an hour.

I don't have to say so because people can see it from leagues away: I'm ugly, shy, and anachronistic. But by dint of not wanting to be those things I have pretended to be just the opposite. Until today, when I have resolved to tell of my own free will just what I'm like, if only to ease my conscience. I have begun with my unusual call to Rosa Cabarcas because, seen from the vantage point of today, that was the beginning of a new life at an age when most mortals have already died.

I live in a colonial house, on the sunny side of San Nicolás Park, where I have spent all the days of my life without wife or fortune, where my parents lived and died, and where I have proposed to die alone, in the same bed in which I was born and on a day that I hope will be distant and painless. My father bought the house at public auction at the end of the nineteenth century, rented the ground floor for luxury shops to a consortium of Italians, and reserved for himself the second floor, where he would live in happiness with one of their daughters, Florina de Dios Cargamantos, a notable interpreter of Mozart, a multilingual Garibaldian, and the most beautiful and talented woman who ever lived in the city: my mother.

The house is spacious and bright, with stucco arches and floors tiled in Florentine mosaics, and four glass doors leading to a wraparound balcony where my mother would sit on March nights to sing love arias with other girls, her cousins. From there you can see San Nicolás Park, the cathedral, and the statue of Christopher Columbus, and beyond that the warehouses on the river wharf and the vast horizon of the Great Magdalena River twenty leagues distant from its estuary. The only unpleasant aspect of the house is that the sun keeps changing windows in the course of the day, and all of them have to be closed when you try to take a siesta in the torrid half-light. When I was left on my own, at the age of thirty-two, I moved into what had been my parents' bedroom, opened a doorway between that room and the library, and began to auction off whatever I didn't need to live, which turned out to be almost everything but the books and the Pianola rolls.

For forty years I was the cable editor at *El Diario de La Paz*, which meant reconstructing and completing in indigenous prose the news of the world that we caught as it flew through sidereal space on shortwaves or in Morse code. Today I scrape by on my pension from that extinct profession, get by even less on the one I receive for having taught Spanish and Latin grammar, earn almost nothing from the Sunday column I've written without flagging for more than half a century, and nothing at all from the music and theater pieces published as a favor to me on the many occasions when notable performers come to town. I have never done anything except write, but I don't possess the vocation or talents of a narrator, have no knowledge at all of the laws of dramatic composition, and if I have embarked upon this enterprise it is because I trust in the light shed by how much I have read in my life. In plain language, I am the end of a line, without merit or brilliance, who would have nothing to leave his descendants if not for the events I am prepared to recount, to the best of my ability, in these memories of my great love.

On my ninetieth birthday I woke, as always, at five in the morning. Since it was Friday, my only obligation was to write the signed column published on Sundays in *El Diario de La Paz*. My symptoms at dawn were perfect for not feeling happy: my bones had been aching since the small hours, my asshole burned, and thunder threatened a storm after three months of drought. I bathed while the coffee was brewing, drank a large cup sweetened with honey, had two pieces of cassava bread, and put on the linen coverall I wear in the house.

The subject of that day's column, of course, was my ninetieth birthday. I never have thought about age as a leak in the roof indicating the quantity of life one has left to live. When I was very young I heard someone say that when people die the lice nesting in their hair escape in terror onto the pillows, to the shame of the family. That was so harsh a warning to me that I let my hair be shorn for school, and the few strands I have left I still wash with the soap you would use on a grateful fleabitten dog. This means, I tell myself now, that ever since I was little my sense of social decency has been more developed than my sense of death.

For months I had anticipated that my birthday column would not be the usual lament for the years that were gone, but just the opposite: a glorification of old age. I began by wondering when I had become aware of being old, and I believe it was only a short time before that day. At the age of forty-two I had gone to see the doctor about a pain in my back that interfered with my breathing. He attributed no importance to it: That kind of pain is natural at your age, he said.

"In that case," I said, "what isn't natural is my age."

The doctor gave me a pitying smile. I see that you're a philosopher, he said. It was the first time I thought about my age in terms of being old, but it didn't take me long to forget about it. I became accustomed to waking every day with a different pain that kept changing location and form as the years passed. At times it seemed to be the clawing of death, and the next day it would disappear. This was when I heard that the first symptom of old age is when you begin to resemble your father. I must be condemned to eternal youth, I thought, because my equine profile will never look like my father's raw Caribbean features or my mother's imperial Roman ones. The truth is that the first changes are so slow they pass almost unnoticed, and you go on seeing yourself as you always were, from the inside, but others observe you from the outside.

In my fifth decade I had begun to imagine what old age was like when I noticed the first lapses of memory. I would turn the house upside down looking for my glasses until I discovered that I had them on, or I'd wear them into the shower, or I'd put on my reading glasses over the ones I used for distance. One day I had breakfast twice because I forgot about the first time, and I learned to recognize the alarm in my friends when they didn't have the courage to tell me I was recounting the same story I had told them a week earlier. By then I had a mental list of faces I knew and another list of the names that went with each one, but at the moment of greeting I didn't always succeed in matching the faces to the names.

My sexual age never worried me because my powers did not depend so much on me as on women, and they know the how and the why when they want to. Today I laugh at the eighty-year-old youngsters who consult the doctor, alarmed by these sudden shocks, not knowing that in your nineties they're worse but don't matter anymore: they are the risks of being alive. On the other hand, it is a triumph of life that old people lose their memories of inessential things, though memory does not often fail with regard to things that are of real interest to us. Cicero illustrated this with the stroke of a pen: *No old man forgets where he has hidden his treasure.*

With these reflections, and several others, I had finished a first draft of my column when the August sun exploded among the almond trees in the park, and the riverboat that carried the mail, a week late because of the drought, came bellowing into the port canal. I thought: My ninetieth birthday is arriving. I'll never know why, and don't pretend to, but it was under the magical effect of that devastating evocation that I decided to call Rosa Cabarcas for help in celebrating my birthday with a libertine night. I'd spent years at holy peace with my body, devoting my time to the erratic rereading of my classics and to my private programs of concert music, but my desire that day was so urgent it seemed like a message from God. After the call I couldn't go on writing. I hung the hammock in a corner of the library where the sun doesn't shine in the morning, and I lay down in it, my chest heavy with the anxiety of waiting.

I had been a pampered child, with a mother of many talents who died of consumption at the age of fifty and a formalistic father who never acknowledged an error and died in his widower's bed on the day the Treaty of Neerlandia was signed, putting an end to the War of the Thousand Days and the countless civil wars of the previous century. Peace changed the city in a way that had not been foreseen or desired. A crowd of free women enriched to the point of delirium the old taverns along Calle Anche, which later was known as Camellón Abello, and now is called Paseo Colón, in this city of my soul loved so much by both natives and outsiders for the good character of its people and the purity of its light.

I have never gone to bed with a woman I didn't pay, and the few who weren't in the profession I persuaded, by argument or by force, to take money even if they threw it in the trash. When I was twenty I began to keep a record listing name, age, place, and a brief notation on the circumstances and style of lovemaking. By the time I was fifty there were 514 women with whom I had been at least once. I stopped making the list when my body no longer allowed me to have so many and I could keep track of them without paper. I had my own ethics. I never took part in orgies or in public encounters, and I did not share secrets or recount an adventure of the body or the soul, because from the time I was young I realized that none goes unpunished.

The only unusual relationship was the one I maintained for years with the faithful Damiana. She was almost a girl, Indianlike, strong, rustic, her words few and brusque, who went barefoot so as not to disturb me while I was writing. I remember I was reading *La lozana andaluza—The Haughty Andalusian Girl—* in the hammock in the hallway, when I happened to see her bending over in the laundry room wearing a skirt so short it bared her succulent curves. Overcome by irresistible excitement, I pulled her skirt up in back, pulled her underwear down to her knees, and charged her from behind. Oh, Señor, she said, with a mournful lament, that wasn't made for coming in but for going out. A profound tremor shook her body but she stood firm. Humiliated at having humiliated her, I wanted to pay her twice what the most expensive women cost at the time, but she would not take a cent, and I had to raise her salary calculated on the basis of one mounting a month, always while she was doing the laundry, and always from the back.

At one time I thought these bed-inspired accounts would serve as a good foundation for a narration of the miseries of my misguided life, and the title came to me out of the blue: Memories of My Melancholy Whores. My public life, on the other hand, was lacking in interest: both parents dead, a bachelor without a future, a mediocre journalist who had been a finalist four times in the Poetic Competition, the Juegos Florales, of Cartagena de Indias, and a favorite of caricaturists because of my exemplary ugliness. In short, a wasted life off to a bad start beginning on the afternoon my mother led me by the hand when I was nineteen years old to see if El Diario de La Paz would publish a chronicle of school life that I had written in my Spanish and rhetoric class. It was published on Sunday with an encouraging introduction by the editor. Years later, when I learned that my mother had paid for its publication and for the seven that followed, it was too late for me to be embarrassed, because my weekly column was flying on its own wings and I was a cable editor and music critic as well.

After I obtained my *bachillerato* with a diploma ranked excellent, I began teaching classes in Spanish and Latin at three different public secondary schools at the same time. I was a poor teacher, with no training, no vocation, and no pity at all for those poor children who attended school as the easiest way to escape the tyranny of their parents. The only thing I could do for them was to keep them subject to the terror of my wooden ruler so that at least they would take away with them my favorite poem: *O Fabio, O sorrow, what you see now, these fields of desolation, gloomy hills, were once the famous fair Italica.* Only as an old man did I happen to learn the nasty name the students called me behind my back: Professor Gloomy Hills.

This was all that life gave me, and I have never done anything to obtain more. I ate lunch alone between classes, and at six in the evening I would go to the editorial offices of the paper to hunt for signals from sidereal space. At eleven, when the edition closed, my real life began. I slept in the red-light district, the Barrio Chino, two or three times a week, and with such a variety of companions that I was twice crowned client of the year. After supper at the nearby Café Roma I would choose a brothel at random and slip in through the back door. I did this because it amused me to, but in the end it became part of my work thanks to the careless speech of political bigwigs who would tell state secrets to their lovers for the night, never thinking they were overheard by public opinion through the cardboard partitions. By this means, of course, I also learned that they attributed my inconsolable bachelorhood to a nocturnal pederasty satisfied by orphan boys on the Calle del Crimen. I had the good fortune to forget this, among other sound reasons because I also heard the positive things said about me, which I appreciated for their true value.

I never had intimate friends, and the few who came close are in New York. By which I mean they're dead, because that's where I suppose condemned souls go in order not to endure the truth of their past lives. Since my retirement I have had little to do except take my pieces to the paper on Friday afternoons or fulfill other obligations that have a certain significance: concerts at Bellas Artes, painting exhibitions at the Centro Artístico, of which I am a founding member, an occasional civic conference at the Society for Public Improvement, or an important event like Fábregas's engagement at the Teatro Apolo. As a young man I would go to the open-air movie theaters, where we could be surprised by a lunar eclipse or by a case of double pneumonia from a downpour gone astray. But what interested me more than films were the little birds of the night who would go to bed with you for the price of a ticket, or at no cost, or on credit. Movies are not my genre. The obscene cult of Shirley Temple was the final straw.

My only travels were four trips to the Juegos Florales in Cartagena de Indias, before I was thirty, and a bad night aboard a motor launch, when I was invited by Sacramento Montiel to the inauguration of one of her brothels in Santa Marta. As for my domestic life, I don't eat very much and am easy to please. When Damiana grew old she stopped cooking for me, and since then my only regular meal has been a potato omelet at the Café Roma after the paper closes.

And so, on the eve of my ninetieth birthday, I had no lunch and could not concentrate on reading as I waited to hear from Rosa Cabarcas. The cicadas were chirruping as loud as they could in the two-o'clock heat, and the sun's journey past the open windows forced me to move the hammock three times.

It always seemed to me that my birthday fell at the hottest time of the year, and I had learned to tolerate it, but my mood that day made this difficult. At four o'clock I tried to calm my spirit with Johann Sebastian Bach's six Suites for Unaccompanied Cello in the definitive performance by Don Pablo Casals. I consider them the most accomplished pieces in all of music, but instead of soothing me as usual they left me in an even worse state of prostration. I fell asleep during the second, which I think lags somewhat, and in my sleep I confused the cello's lament with that of a melancholy ship that was leaving. At almost the same time the telephone woke me, and the rusted voice of Rosa Cabarcas brought me back to life. You have a fool's luck, she said. I found a little thing even better than what you wanted, but there's one drawback: she just turned fourteen. I don't mind changing diapers, I said as a joke, not understanding her motives. I'm not worried about you, she said, but who's going to pay me for three years in jail?

Nobody was going to pay for them, she least of all, of course. She harvested her crop among the minors for sale in her shop, girls she broke in and squeezed dry until they moved on to a worse life as graduate whores in the historic brothel of Black Eufemia. She had never paid a fine, because her courtyard was the arcadia of local officialdom, from the governor to the lowest hanger-on in the mayor's office, and it was inconceivable that the owner would not have the power to break the law to her heart's content. Which meant her last-minute scruples were intended only to derive profit from her favors: the more punishable they were, the more expensive they would be. The question was settled with a two-peso increase in fees, and we agreed that at ten that night I would be at her house with five pesos in cash, payable in advance. Not a minute earlier, since the girl had to feed her younger brothers and sisters and put them to sleep and help her mother, crippled by rheumatism, into bed.

There were four hours to wait. As they passed, my heart filled with an acidic foam that interfered with my breathing. I made a useless effort to help time along with the procedures of dressing. Not surprising, of course, if even Damiana says I dress with all the rituals of a bishop. I shaved with my barber's straight razor and had to wait until the water for the shower cooled, because it had been heated in the pipes by the sun, and the simple effort of drying myself with the towel made me sweat all over again. I dressed in accordance with the night's good fortune:

a white linen suit, a blue-striped shirt with a collar stiffened by starch, a tie of Chinese silk, boots rejuvenated with zinc white, and a watch of fine gold, its chain fastened at the buttonhole on my lapel. Then I folded the trouser cuffs under so that no one would notice the inches I've shrunk.

I have a reputation as a miser because no one can imagine I'm as poor as I am if I live where I live, but the truth is that a night like this was far beyond my means. From the money box hidden under my bed I took out two pesos to rent the room, four for the owner, three for the girl, and five in reserve for my supper and other minor expenses. In other words, the fourteen pesos the paper pays me for a month of Sunday columns. I hid them in a secret pocket inside my waistband, and I sprayed on the Florida Water of Lanman & Kemp-Barclay & Co. Then I felt the clawing of panic, and at the first stroke of eight I groped my way down the dark stairs, sweating with fear, and went out into the radiant night before my birthday.

The weather had cooled. On the Paseo Colón groups of men were arguing at the top of their voices about soccer among the array of taxis parked in the middle of the sidewalk. A brass band played a languid waltz under the alameda of blossoming *matarratón* trees. One of the poor little whores who hunt solemn clients on the Calle de los Notarios asked me for the usual cigarette, and I gave my usual answer: Today it's thirty-three years, two months, and seventeen days since I stopped smoking. When I passed El Alambre de Oro I glanced at myself in the lighted windows, and I didn't look the way I felt but older, dressed in shabbier clothes.

A little before ten I climbed into a taxi and asked the driver to take me to the Cementerio Universal so he wouldn't know where I was really going. Amused, he looked at me in the mirror and said: Don't scare me like that, Don Scholar, I hope God keeps me as alive as you are. We got out together in front of the cemetery because he didn't have change and we had to get some in La Tumba, a destitute tavern where the poor drunkards of the small hours weep for their dead. When we had settled accounts, the driver said to me in a serious voice: Be careful, Señor, Rosa Cabarcas's house isn't even a shadow of what it was. All I could do was thank him, convinced, like everyone else, that there was no secret under the sun for the drivers on Paseo Colón.

I walked into a poor district that had nothing to do with the one I had known in my day. It had the same wide streets of hot sand, houses with open doors, walls of rough wooden planks, roofs of bitter palm, and gravel courtyards. But its people had lost their tranquility. In most of the houses there were wild Friday parties with drums and cymbals that reverberated in your gut. For fifty centavos anybody could go into the party he liked best, but he could also stay outside and dance on the sidewalk to the music. I walked, worried the earth would swallow me up in my dandy's outfit, but nobody paid attention to me except for an emaciated mulatto who sat dozing in the doorway of a tenement house.

"Go with God, Doctor," he shouted with all his heart, "and happy fucking!"

What could I do but thank him? I had to stop at least three times to catch my breath before I reached the top of the last incline. From there I saw the enormous copper moon coming up at the horizon, and an unexpected urgency in the belly made me fearful of the outcome, but that passed soon enough. At the end of the street, where the neighborhood turned into a forest of fruit trees, I went into Rosa Cabarcas's shop.

She didn't look the same. She had been the most discreet madam and for that same reason the best known, a very large woman whom we had wanted to crown as a sergeant in the fire department, as much for her corpulence as for her efficiency in putting out fires among her clientele. But solitude had shrunk her body, withered her skin, and sharpened her voice with so much skill that she resembled an aged little girl. All that was left to her from the old days were her perfect teeth, along with one she had capped with gold for coquettish reasons. She dressed in strict mourning for the husband who had died after fifty years of a shared life, added to which was a kind of black bonnet for the death of her only child, who used to assist her in her illicit activities. Only her clear, cruel eyes were still animated, and because of them I realized her character had not changed.

The shop had a dim lightbulb hanging from the ceiling and almost nothing for sale on the shelves, which did not even serve as a screen for a notorious business that everyone knew about but no one acknowledged. Rosa Cabarcas was taking care of a client when I tiptoed in. I don't know if she really did not recognize me or if she was pretending for the sake of appearances. I sat on a bench to wait while she finished up, and in my memory I tried to reconstruct her as she had been. More than a few times, when both of us were strong and healthy, she had saved me from my own delusions. I think she read my mind because she turned toward me and scrutinized me with alarming intensity. Time doesn't go by for you, and she heaved a mournful sigh. I wanted to flatter her: It does for you, but it makes you better. I'm serious, she said, it's even helped to revive your dead horse's face a little. It must be because I changed brothels, I said to tease her. She became animated. As I remember, you had the tool of a galley slave, she said. How's it behaving? I evaded the question: The only thing different since the last time we saw each other is that sometimes my asshole burns. Her diagnosis was immediate: Lack of use. I have it only for the use God intended, I said, but it was true that it had burned for some time, always when the moon was full. Rosa searched through her sewing kit and opened a little tin of green salve that smelled of arnica liniment. You tell the girl to rub it in with her finger, like this, and she moved her index finger with brazen eloquence. I replied that thanks be to God I was still capable of getting along without peasant ointments. She mocked me, saying: Ah, Maestro, excuse me for living. And turned to business.

The girl had been in the room since ten, she told me; she was beautiful, clean, and well-mannered, but dying of fear because a friend of hers who ran away with a stevedore from Gayra had bled to death in two hours. But then, Rosa admitted, it's understandable because the men from Gayra are famous for making she-mules sing. And she returned to her subject: Poor thing, besides all that she has to work the whole day attaching buttons in a factory. It didn't seem to me like such hard work. That's what men think, she replied, but it's worse than breaking rocks. She went on to confess that she had given the girl a mixture of bromide and valerian to drink, and now she was asleep. I was afraid her compassion might be another trick to raise the price, but no, she said, my word is as good as gold. With set rules: each thing requiring separate payment, in cash and in advance. And so it was.

I followed her across the courtyard, moved by her wrinkled skin and the difficulty she had walking because of her swollen legs, encased in heavy cotton stockings. The full moon was climbing to the middle of the sky and the world looked as if it were submerged in green water. Near the shop was a canopy made of palm for the wild revels held by public administrators, with a good number of leather stools, and hammocks hanging from the wooden columns. In the back courtyard, where the forest of fruit trees began, there was a gallery of six unplastered adobe rooms with burlap windows to keep out mosquitoes. The only one that was occupied had a dim light and Toña la Negra singing a song of failed love on the radio. Rosa Cabarcas sighed: The bolero is life. I agreed, but until today I haven't dared write it. She pushed the door, went in for a moment, and came out again. She's still asleep, she said. You ought to let her rest for as long as her body needs it, your night is longer than hers. I was bewildered: What do you think I should do? You ought to know, she said with unwarranted placidity, there's *some* reason you're a scholar. She turned and left me alone with my terror.

There was no escape. I went into the room, my heart in confusion, and saw the girl sleeping in the enormous bed for hire, as naked and helpless as the day she was born. She lay on her side, facing the door, illuminated from the ceiling by an intense light that spared no detail. I sat down to contemplate her from the edge of the bed, my five senses under a spell. She was dark and warm. She had been subjected to a regimen of hygiene and beautification that did not overlook even the incipient down on her pubis. Her hair had been curled, and she wore natural polish on the nails of her fingers and toes, but her molasses-colored skin looked rough and mistreated. Her newborn breasts still seemed like a boy's, but they appeared full to bursting with a secret energy that was ready to explode. The best part of her body were her large, silent-stepping feet with toes as long and sensitive as fingers. She was drenched in phosphorescent perspiration despite the fan, and the heat became unbearable as the night progressed. It was impossible to imagine what her face was like under the paint applied with a heavy hand, the thick layer of rice powder with two daubs of rouge on her cheeks, the false lashes, her eyebrows and lids smoky with kohl, her lips augmented by a chocolate glaze. But the adornments and cosmetics could not hide her character: the haughty nose, heavy eyebrows, intense lips. I thought: A tender young fighting bull.

At eleven I tended to my routine procedures in the bathroom, where the poor girl's clothes were folded on a chair with a rich girl's refinement: an etamine dress with a butterfly print, cheap yellow panties, and fiber sandals. On top of the clothing were an inexpensive bracelet and a very fine chain with a medal of the Virgin. On the edge of the sink, a handbag with a lipstick, a compact of rouge, a key, and some loose coins. Everything so cheap and shabby with use that I couldn't imagine anyone as poor as she was.

I undressed and did my best to arrange my clothes on the hanger so as not to muss the silk shirt and pressed linen. I urinated in the chain-flush toilet, sitting down as Florina de Dios had taught me to do from the time I was a boy so I would not wet the rim of the bowl, and still, modesty aside, with the immediate, steady stream of an untamed colt. Before I went out I peered into the mirror over the sink. The horse that looked back at me from the other side was not dead but funereal, and he had a Pope's dewlaps, puffy eyelids, and thin, lank hair that had once been my musician's mane.

"Shit," I said to him, "what can I do if you don't love me?"

Trying not to wake her, I sat on the bed, naked, my eyes accustomed by now to the deceptions of the red light, and I scrutinized her inch by inch. I ran the tip of my index finger along the damp nape of her neck, and she shivered inside, along the length of her body, like a chord on the harp, turned toward me with a grumble, and enveloped me in the ambience of her acid breath. I pinched her nose with my thumb and index finger, and she shook herself, moved her head away, and turned her back to me without waking. I succumbed to an unforeseen temptation and tried to separate her legs with my knee. On the first two attempts, she resisted with tensed thighs. I sang into her ear: *Angels surround the bed of Delgadina.* She relaxed a little. A warm current traveled up my veins, and my slow, retired animal woke from its long sleep.

Delgadina, my heart, I pleaded, filled with longing. Delgadina. She gave a sorrowful moan, escaped my thighs, turned her back, and curled up like a snail in its shell. The valerian potion must have been as effective for me as for her, because nothing happened, not to her, not to anybody. But I didn't care. I asked myself what good it would do to wake her when I was feeling humiliated and sad and as cold as a striped mullet.

Then the bells, clear and ineluctable, struck midnight, and the morning of August 29, the day of the Martyrdom of St. John the Baptist, began. Someone in the street wept at the top of his lungs and no one paid attention. I prayed for him, in case he needed that, and for me as well, giving thanks for benefits received: *Let no one be deceived, no, thinking that what he awaits will last longer than what he has seen.* The girl moaned in her sleep and I also prayed for her: *For everything will pass in its turn*. Then I turned off the radio and the light and went to sleep.

I woke in the small hours, not remembering where I was. The girl still slept in a fetal position, her back to me. I had a vague feeling that I had sensed her getting up in the dark and had heard water running in the bathroom, but it might have been a dream. This was something new for me. I was ignorant of the arts of seduction and had always chosen my brides for a night at random, more for their price than their charms, and we had made love without love, half-dressed most of the time and always in the dark so we could imagine ourselves as better than we were. That night I discovered the improbable pleasure of contemplating the body of a sleeping woman without the urgencies of desire or the obstacles of modesty.

I got up at five, uneasy because my Sunday column was supposed to be on the editor's desk before noon. I moved my punctual bowels, still with the burning of the full moon, and when I pulled the chain I felt that my past rancors had gone down to the sewer. When I returned to the bedroom, refreshed and dressed, the girl was asleep on her back in the conciliatory light of dawn, lying sideways across the bed with her arms opened in a cross, absolute mistress of her virginity. God bless you, I said to her. All the money I still had, both hers and mine, I put on the pillow, and I said goodbye forever with a kiss on her forehead. The house, like all brothels at dawn, was the closest thing to paradise. I left by the orchard gate so I wouldn't meet anyone. Under the burning sun on the street I began to feel the weight of my ninety years, and to count minute by minute the minutes of the nights I had left before I died.

2

I AM WRITING these memories in the little that remains of the library that belonged to my parents, and whose shelves are about to collapse as a result of the patience of bookworms. When all is said and done, for what I still have left to do in this world, I'd be satisfied with my many kinds of dictionaries, the first two series of the *Episodios nacionales* by Don Benito Pérez Galdós, and *The Magic Mountain*, which taught me to understand my mother's moods, distorted by consumption.

Unlike the rest of the furniture, and unlike me, the large table on which I am writing seems to grow healthier with the passage of time, because my paternal grandfather, a ship's carpenter, fashioned it from noble woods. Even when I don't have to write, I arrange it every morning with the pointless rigor that has made me lose so many lovers. Within reach I have the books that are my accomplices: the two volumes of the *Primer diccionario ilustrado* of the Royal Academy, dated 1903; the *Tesoro de la lengua castellana o española* of Don Sebastián de Covarrubias; Don Andrés Bello's grammar, essential in the event I have a semantic question; the innovative *Diccionario ideológico* by Don Julio Casares, in particular for its antonyms and synonyms; the *Vocabolario della lingua italiana*, by Nicola Zingarelli, to help me with my mother's language, which I learned in the cradle; and a Latin dictionary: since it is the mother of the other two, I consider it my native tongue.

On the left side of the writing table I always keep five sheets of office-size rag paper for my Sunday column, and the horn with sand to dry the ink, which I prefer to the modern pad of blotting paper. On the right are the inkwell and holder of light balsa wood with its gold pen, for I still write in the romantic hand that Florina de Dios taught me so I would not adopt the functionary's handwriting of her husband, who was a public notary and certified accountant until he drew his final breath. Some time ago the newspaper

ordered everyone to type in order to improve esti-
mates of the text in the linotype's lead and achieve
greater accuracy in typesetting, but I never adopted
that bad habit. I continued to write by hand and to
transcribe on the typewriter with a hen's arduous
pecking, thanks to the unwanted privilege of being
the oldest employee. Today, retired but not defeated,
I enjoy the sacred privilege of writing at home, with
the phone off the hook so that no one can disturb me,
and without a censor looking over my shoulder to see
what I am writing.

I live without dogs or birds or servants, except for
the faithful Damiana who has rescued me from the
most unexpected difficulties, and who still comes once
a week to take care of whatever there is to do, even in
the state she is in, losing her sight and her acumen.
My mother on her deathbed asked me to marry a fair-
skinned woman while I was young and have at least
three children, one of them a girl with her name,
which had also been her mother's and grandmother's.
I intended to comply with her request, but my notion
of youth was so flexible I never thought it was too
late. Until one hot afternoon when I opened the
wrong door in the house of the Palomar de Cas-
tro family in Pradomar and saw Ximena Ortiz, the

youngest of the daughters, naked as she took her siesta in the adjoining bedroom. She was lying with her back to the door, and she turned to look at me over her shoulder with a gesture so rapid it didn't give me time to escape. Oh, excuse me, I managed to say, my heart in my mouth. She smiled, turned toward me with the grace of a gazelle, and showed me her entire body. The whole room felt saturated with her intimacy. Her nakedness was not absolute, for like Manet's *Olympia*, behind her ear she had a poisonous flower with orange petals, and she also wore a gold bangle on her right wrist and a necklace of tiny pearls. I imagined I would never see anything more exciting for as long as I lived, and today I can confirm that I was right.

I slammed the door shut, embarrassed by my blundering and determined to forget her. But Ximena Ortiz prevented that. She sent me messages with mutual friends, provocative notes, brutal threats, while she spread the rumor that we were mad with love for each other though we hadn't exchanged a word. She was impossible to resist. She had the eyes of a wildcat, a body as provocative with clothes as without, and luxuriant hair of uproarious gold whose woman's smell made me weep with rage into my pillow. I knew it would never turn into love, but the satanic attraction she held for me was so fiery that I attempted to find relief with every green-eyed tart I came across. I never could put out the flame of her memory in the bed at Pradomar, and so I surrendered my weapons to her with a formal request for her hand, an exchange of rings, and the announcement of a large wedding before Pentecost.

The news exploded with greater impact in the Barrio Chino than in the social clubs. At first it was met with derision, but this changed into absolute vexation on the part of those erudite women who viewed marriage as a condition more ridiculous than sacred. My engagement satisfied all the rituals of Christian morality on the terrace, with its Amazonian orchids and hanging ferns, of my fiancée's house. I would arrive at seven in the evening dressed all in white linen, with a gift of handcrafted beads or Swiss chocolates, and we would talk, half in code and half in seriousness, until ten, watched over by Aunt Argénida, who fell asleep in the blink of an eye, like the chaperones in the novels of the day.

Ximena became more voracious the better we got to know each other, she would loosen her bodices and petticoats as the sultry heat of June increased, and it was easy to imagine the devastating power she would have in the dark. After two months of being engaged we had nothing left to talk about, and without saying anything she brought up the subject of children by crocheting little boots for newborns from raw wool. I, the agreeable fiancé, learned to crochet with her, and in this way we passed the useless hours until the wedding: I crocheted little blue booties for boys and she crotcheted pink ones for girls, we'd see who guessed right, until there were enough for more than fifty babies. Before the clock struck ten, I would climb into a horse-drawn carriage and go to the Barrio Chino to live my night in the peace of God.

The tempestuous farewells to bachelorhood that they gave me in the Barrio Chino were the opposite of the oppressive evenings at the Social Club. A contrast that helped me find out which of the two worlds in reality was mine, and I hoped that both were, each at its proper time, because from either one I would watch the other moving away with the heartrending sighs of two ships passing at sea. On the night before the wedding, the dance at El Poder de Dios included a final ceremony that could have occurred only to a Galician priest foundering in concupiscence, who dressed the entire female staff in veils and orange blossoms so that all of them would marry me in a universal sacrament. It was a night of great sacrileges in which twenty-two women promised love and obedience and I reciprocated with fidelity and support for as long as we lived.

I could not sleep because of a presentiment of something irremediable. In the middle of the night I began to count the passage of the hours on the cathedral clock, until the seven dreadful bells when I was supposed to be at the church. The telephone began to ring at eight, long, tenacious, unpredictable rings for more than an hour. Not only did I not answer: I did not breathe. A little before ten someone knocked at the door, first a fist pounding and then the shouting of voices I knew and despised. I was afraid they would push down the door in some serious mishap, but by eleven the house was left in the bristling silence that follows great catastrophes. Then I wept for her and for me, and I prayed with all my heart never to see her again in all my days. Some saint half-heard me, because Ximena Ortiz left the country that same night and did not return until twenty years later, married and with seven children who could have been mine.

It was difficult for me to keep my position and

my column at *El Diario de La Paz* after that social affront. It wasn't because of this, however, that they relegated my columns to page eleven, but because of the blind impetus with which the twentieth century came on the scene. Progress became the myth of the city. Everything changed; planes flew, and a businessman tossed a sack of letters out of a Junker and invented airmail.

The only things that remained the same were my columns in the newspaper. Younger generations launched an attack against them as if they were assaulting a mummy from the past that had to be destroyed, but I maintained the same tone and made no concessions to the winds of renovation. I remained deaf to everything. I had turned forty, but the young staff writers named it the Column of Mudarra the Bastard. The editor at the time called me into his office to ask me to conform to the latest currents. In a solemn way, as if he had just thought of it, he said: The world is moving ahead. Yes, I said, it's moving ahead, but it's revolving around the sun. He kept my Sunday column because he could not have found another cable editor. Today I know I was right, and I know why. The adolescents of my generation, greedy for life, forgot in body and soul about their hopes for the future until reality taught them that tomorrow was not what they had dreamed, and they discovered nostalgia. My Sunday columns were there, like an archeological relic among the ruins of the past, and they realized they were not only for the old but also for the young who were not afraid of aging. Then the column returned to the editorial section and, on special occasions, to the front page.

Whenever someone asks I always answer with the truth: whores left me no time to be married. Still, I should acknowledge that I did not come up with this explanation until the day of my ninetieth birthday, when I left Rosa Cabarcas's house determined never again to provoke fate. I felt like a different man. My mood was upset by the disreputable mob I saw leaning against the metal railings around the park. I found Damiana washing the floor, on all fours in the living room, and the youthfulness of her thighs at her age revived in me a tremor from another time. She must have sensed it because she covered herself with her skirt. I could not resist the temptation to ask: Tell me something, Damiana: what do you recall? I wasn't recalling anything, she said, but your question makes me remember. I felt a weight in my chest. I've never fallen in love, I told her. She replied without hesitation: I have. And she concluded, not interrupting her work: I cried over you for twenty-two years. My heart skipped a beat. Looking for a dignified way out, I said: We would have made a good team. Well, it's wrong of you to say so now, she said, because you're no good to me anymore even as a consolation. As she was leaving the house, she said in the most natural way: You won't believe me but thanks be to God, I'm still a virgin.

A short while later I discovered that she had left vases filled with red roses all over the house, and a card on my pillow: *I hope you reach a hunnert*. With this bad taste in my mouth I sat down to continue the column I had left half-finished the day before. I completed it without stopping in less than two hours and had to "twist the neck of the swan," as the Mexican poet said, to write from my heart and not have anyone notice my tears. In a belated moment of inspiration, I decided to finish it with the announcement that with this column I was bringing to a happy conclusion a long and worthy life without the sad necessity of having to die.

My intention was to leave it with reception at the paper and return home. But I couldn't. The entire staff was waiting for me in order to celebrate my birthday. The building was being renovated, and scaffolding and rubble were everywhere, but they had stopped work for the party. On a carpenter's table were drinks for the toast and birthday presents wrapped in gift paper. Dazed by flashing cameras, I was included in every photograph taken as a memento.

I was glad to see radio newscasters and reporters from other papers in the city: *La Prensa*, the conservative morning paper, *El Heraldo*, the liberal morning paper, and *El Nacional*, the evening sensationalist tabloid that always tried to relieve tensions in the public order with serialized stories of passion. It wasn't strange that they were together, for in the spirit of the city it was always considered good form to maintain friendships among the troops while the officers waged editorial war.

Also present, though not at his regular hours, was the official censor, Don Jerónimo Ortega, whom we called the Abominable No-Man because he would arrive with his reactionary satrap's blood-red pencil at nine sharp every night and stay until he was certain no letter in the morning edition went unpunished. He had a personal aversion to me, either because of my grammarian's airs or because I would use Italian words without quotation marks or italics when they seemed more expressive than Spanish, which ought to be legitimate practice between Siamese languages. After enduring him for four years, we had come to accept him in the end as our own bad conscience.

The secretaries brought in a cake with ninety lit candles that confronted me for the first time with the number of my years. I had to swallow tears when they sang the birthday song, and for no reason I thought about the girl. It wasn't a flash of rancor but of belated compassion for a creature I had not expected to think about again. When the moment passed someone had placed a knife in my hand so that I could cut the cake. For fear of being laughed at, no one risked improvising a speech. I would rather have died than respond to one. To conclude the party, the editor in chief, whom I had never liked very much, returned us to harsh reality. And now, illustrious nonagenarian, he said to me: Where's your column?

The truth is that all afternoon I had felt it burning in my pocket like a live coal, but emotion had pierced me in so profound a way I did not have the heart to spoil the party with my resignation. I said: On this occasion there is none. The editor in chief was annoyed at a lapse that had been inconceivable since the previous century. Understand just this once, I said, I had so difficult a night I woke up in a stupor. Well, you should have written about that, he said with his vinegary humor. Readers would like to know firsthand what life is like at ninety. One of the secretaries intervened. It must be a delicious secret, she said and gave me a mischievous look: Isn't it? A burning flash flamed across my face. Damn it, I thought, blushing is so disloyal. Another radiant secretary pointed at me with her finger. How wonderful! You still have the elegance to blush. Her impertinence provoked another blush on top of the first. It must have been a phenomenal night, said the first secretary: How I envy you! And she gave me a kiss that left its painted mark on my face. The photographers were merciless. Bewildered, I gave the column to the editor in chief and told him that what I had said before was a joke, here it is, and I escaped, confused by the last round of applause, in order not to be present when they discovered it was my letter of resignation after half a century of galleys.

I was still apprehensive that night when I unwrapped the presents at home. The linotypists had miscalculated with an electric coffeepot just like the three I had from previous birthdays. The typographers gave me an authorization to pick up an angora cat at the municipal animal shelter. Management bestowed on me a symbolic bonus. The secretaries presented me with three pairs of silk undershorts printed with kisses, and a card in which they offered to remove them for me. It occurred to me that among the charms of old age are the provocations our young female friends permit themselves because they think we are out of commission.

I never found out how I got a record of Chopin's twenty-four Preludes played by Stefan Askenase. Most of the writers gave me best-selling books. I hadn't finished unwrapping the gifts when Rosa Cabarcas called with the question I did not want to hear: What happened to you with the girl? Nothing, I said without thinking. You think it's nothing when you didn't even wake her up? said Rosa Cabarcas. A woman never forgives a man who treats her debut with contempt. I contended that the girl could not be so exhausted just from attaching buttons, and perhaps she pretended to be asleep out of fear of the perilous moment. The one thing that's serious, said Rosa, is that she really believes you can't anymore, and I wouldn't like her to advertise it.

I didn't give her the satisfaction of showing surprise. Even if that happened, I said, her condition is so deplorable she can't be counted on either asleep or awake: she's a candidate for the hospital. Rosa Cabarcas lowered her voice: The problem was how fast the deal was made, but that can be fixed, you'll see. She promised to bring the girl to confession, and if appropriate oblige her to return the money, what do you think? Leave it alone, I said, nothing happened, in fact it showed me I'm in no condition for this kind of chasing around. In that sense the girl's right: I can't anymore. I hung up the phone, filled with a sense of liberation I hadn't known before in my life, and free at last of a servitude that had kept me enslaved since the age of thirteen.

At seven that evening I was guest of honor at the concert in Bellas Artes by Jacques Thibault and Alfred Cortot, whose interpretation of the Sonata for Violin and Piano by César Franck was glorious, and during the intermission I listened to improbable praise. Maestro Pedro Biava, our gigantic musician, almost dragged me to the dressing rooms to introduce me to the soloists. I was so dazzled I congratulated them for a sonata by Schumann they hadn't played, and someone corrected me in public in an unpleasant fashion. The impression that I had confused the two sonatas out of simple ignorance was sown on the local musical scene and made worse by the muddled explanation with which I tried to correct it the following Sunday in my review of the concert.

For the first time in my long life I felt capable of killing someone. I returned home tormented by the little demon who whispers into our ear the devastating replies we didn't give at the right time, and neither reading nor music could mitigate my rage. It was fortunate that Rosa Cabarcas pulled me out of my madness by shouting into the telephone: I'm happy with the paper because I thought you were turning a hundred, not ninety. I answered in a fury: Did I look that fucked up to you? Not at all, she said, what surprised me was to see you looking so good. I'm glad you're not one of those dirty old men who say they're older so people will think they're in good shape. And with no transition she changed the subject: I have your present for you. I was, in fact, surprised: What is it? The girl, she said.

I didn't need even an instant to think about it. Thanks, I said, but that's water under the bridge. She continued without pausing: I'll send her to your house wrapped in India paper and simmered with sandalwood in the double boiler, all free of charge. I remained firm, and she argued with a stony explanation that seemed sincere. She said the girl had been in such bad condition on Friday because she had sewn two hundred buttons with needle and thimble. And it was true she was afraid of bloody violations but had already been instructed regarding the sacrifice. And during her night with me she had gotten up to go to the bathroom, and I was in such a deep sleep she thought it would be a shame to wake me, but I had already left when she woke again in the morning. I became indignant at what seemed a useless lie. Well, Rosa Cabarcas went on, even if that's so, the girl is sorry. Poor thing, she's right here in front of me. Do you want to talk to her? No, for God's sake, I said.

I had begun writing when the secretary from the paper called. The message was that the editor wanted to see me the next day at eleven in the morning. I was punctual. The din of the renovation work did not seem bearable, the air was rarefied by the sound of hammers, the cement dust, and the steam from tar, but in the editorial room they had learned to think in that routine chaos. On the other hand, the editor's offices, icy and silent, remained in an ideal country that was not ours.

The third Marco Tulio, with his adolescent air,

got to his feet when he saw me come in but did not interrupt his phone conversation, shook my hand across the desk, and indicated that I should sit down. It occurred to me that there was no one on the other end of the line, that he was playing this farce to impress me, but I soon discovered he was talking to the governor and that it was in reality a difficult conversation between cordial enemies. I believe, too, that he took great pains to appear energetic in my presence, though at the same time he remained standing as he spoke to the official.

He had the notable vice of a smart appearance. He had just turned twenty-nine and knew four languages and had three international master's degrees, unlike the first president-for-life, his paternal grandfather, who became an empirical journalist after making a fortune as a white slaver. He had easy manners, unusual good looks and poise, and the only thing that endangered his distinction was a false note in his voice. He was wearing a sports jacket with a live orchid in the lapel, and each article of clothing suited him as if it were part of his natural being, yet nothing was made for the climate of the street but only for the springtime of his offices. I, who had taken almost two hours to dress, felt the ignominy of poverty, and my rage increased.

Still, the mortal poison lay in a panoramic photograph of the staff taken on the twenty-fifth anniversary of the founding of the paper, on which a little cross had been marked above the heads of those who had died. I was third from the right, wearing a straw boater, a large-knotted tie with a pearl tiepin, my first civilian colonel's mustache, which I had until I was forty, and the metal-rimmed glasses of a farsighted seminarian that I hadn't needed after half a century. For years I had seen that photograph hanging in different offices, but it was only then that I became aware of its message: of the forty-eight original employees, only four were still alive, and the youngest of us was serving a twenty-year sentence for multiple homicide.

The editor finished the phone call, caught me looking at the photograph, and smiled. I didn't put in those little crosses, he said. I think they're in very bad taste. He sat down behind his desk and changed his tone: Permit me to say that you are the most unpredictable man I have ever known. And seeing my surprise, he anticipated my response: I say this because of your resignation. I managed to say: It's an entire life. He replied that just for that reason it was not an appropriate solution. He thought the column was magnificent, everything it said about old age was the best he had ever read, and it made no sense to end it with a decision that seemed more like a civil death. It was fortunate, he said, that the editorial page was already put together when the Abominable No-Man read the article and thought it was inadmissible. Without consulting anyone he crossed it out from top to bottom with his Torquemada's pencil. When I found out this morning I had a note of protest sent to the government. It was my duty, but between us, I can say I'm very grateful for the censor's arbitrariness. Which means I was not prepared to accept the termination of the column. I beg you with all my heart, he said. Don't abandon ship in mid ocean. And he concluded in grand style: There is still a great deal left for us to say about music.

He seemed so resolute I did not have the heart to make our disagreement worse with a counter-argument. In fact, the problem was that even on this occasion I could not find a decent reason for abandoning the treadmill, and the idea of once again telling him yes just to gain time terrified me. I had to control myself so he wouldn't notice the shameless emotion bringing tears to my eyes. And again, as always, after so many years we were still in the same place we always were.

The following week, prey to a state closer to confusion than joy, I passed by the animal shelter to pick up the cat the printers had given me. I have very bad chemistry with animals, just as I do with children before they begin to speak. They seem mute in their souls. I don't hate them, but I can't tolerate them, because I never learned to deal with them. I think it is against nature for a man to get along better with his dog than he does with his wife, to teach it to eat and defecate on schedule, to answer his questions and share his sorrows. But not picking up the typographers' cat would have been an insult. Besides, it was a beautiful specimen of an angora, with a rosy, shining coat, bright eyes, and meows that seemed on the verge of being words. They gave him to me in a wicker basket, with a certificate of ancestry and an owner's manual like the one for assembling bicycles.

A military patrol was verifying the identity of pedestrians before allowing them to walk through San Nicolás Park. I had never seen anything like it and could not imagine anything more disheartening as a symptom of my old age. It was a four-man patrol, under the command of an officer who was almost an adolescent. The soldiers were from the highland barrens, hard, silent men who smelled of the stable. The officer kept an eye on all of them with their bright-red cheeks of Andeans at the beach. After looking over my identification papers and press card, he asked what I was carrying in the basket. A cat, I told him. He wanted to see it. I uncovered the basket with as much caution as I could for fear it would escape, but a soldier wanted to see if there was anything else on the bottom, and the cat scratched him. The officer intervened. He's a gem of an angora, he said. He stroked it and murmured something, and the cat didn't attack him but didn't pay any attention to him either. How old is he? he asked. I don't know, I said, it was just given to me. I'm asking because you can see he's very old, perhaps as old as ten. I wanted to ask how he knew, and many other things as well, but in spite of his good manners and flowery speech I didn't have the stomach to talk to him. I think he's an abandoned cat who's gone through a good deal, he said. Observe him, don't try to make him adapt to you, you adapt to him instead, and leave him alone until you gain his confidence. He closed the lid of the basket and asked:

What kind of work do you do? I'm a journalist. How long have you done that? For a century, I told him. I don't doubt it, he said. He shook my hand and said goodbye with a sentence that might have been either good advice or a threat:

"Take good care of yourself."

At noon I disconnected the phone in order to take refuge in an exquisite program of music: Wagner's Rhapsody for Clarinet and Orchestra, Debussy's Rhapsody for Saxophone, and Bruckner's String Quintet, which is an edenic oasis in the cataclysm of his work. And all at once I found myself enveloped in the darkness of the study. Under the table I felt something slip by that did not seem like a living body but a supernatural presence brushing past my feet, and I jumped up with a shout. It was the cat with its beautiful plumed tail, mysterious languor, and mythic ancestry, and I could not help shuddering at being alone in the house with a living being that was not human.

When the cathedral bells struck seven, there was a single, limpid star in the rose-colored sky, a ship called out a disconsolate farewell, and in my throat I felt the Gordian knot of all the loves that might have been and weren't. I could not bear any more. I picked up the phone with my heart in my mouth, dialed the four numbers with slow deliberation in order not to make a mistake, and after the third ring I recognized her voice. All right, woman, I said with a sigh of relief: Forgive my outburst this morning. She was serene: Don't worry about it, I was expecting your call. I told her: I want the girl to wait for me just as God sent her into the world, and with no paint on her face. She laughed her guttural laugh. Whatever you say, she said, but you lose the pleasure of undressing her one piece of clothing at a time, something old men love to do, I don't know why. I do, I said: Because they keep growing older and older. She considered it settled.

"All right," she said, "then tonight at ten sharp, before she has a chance to cool down."

3

WHAT COULD HER NAME BE? The owner hadn't told me. When she talked about her to me she said only: the girl, *la niña*. And I had turned that into a given name, like girl of my dreams, or the smallest of the caravels. Besides, Rosa Cabarcas gave her employees a different name for each client. It amused me to guess their names from their faces, and from the beginning I was sure the girl had a long one, like Filomena, Saturnina, or Nicolasa. I was thinking about this when she gave a half-turn in bed and lay with her back to me, and it looked as if she had left a pool of blood the size and shape of her body. My shock was instantaneous until I confirmed that it was the dampness of her perspiration on the sheet.

Rosa Cabarcas had advised me to treat her with caution, since she still felt her terror of the first time. What is more, I believe the solemnity of the ritual heightened her fear and the dose of valerian had to be increased, for she slept with so much placidity that it would have been a shame to wake her without a lullaby. And so I began to dry her with a towel while I sang in a whisper the song about Delgadina, the king's youngest daughter, wooed by her father. As I dried her she was showing me her sweaty flanks to the rhythm of my song: *Delgadina, Delgadina, you will be my darling love*. It was a limitless pleasure, for she began to perspire again on one side as I finished drying the other, which meant the song might never end. *Arise, arise, Delgadina, and put on your skirt of silk*, I sang into her ear. At the end, when the king's servants find her dead of thirst in her bed, it seemed to me that my girl had been about to wake when she heard the name. Then that's who she was: Delgadina.

I returned to bed wearing my shorts printed with kisses and lay down beside her. I slept until five to the lullaby of her peaceful respiration. I dressed in haste, without washing, and only then did I see the sentence written in lipstick across the mirror over the sink: *The tiger does not eat far away*. I knew it hadn't been there the night before, and no one could have come into the room, and therefore I understood it as a gift from the devil. A terrifying clap of thunder surprised me at the door, and the room filled with the premonitory smell of wet earth. I did not have time to escape untouched. Before I could find a taxi there was a huge downpour, the kind that throws the city into chaos between May and October, for the streets of burning sand that go down to the river turn into gullies formed by the torrents that carry away everything in their path. During that strange September, after three months of drought, the rains could have been as providential as they were devastating.

From the moment I opened the door to my house I was met by the physical sensation that I was not alone. I caught a glimpse of the cat as he jumped off the sofa and raced out to the balcony. In his dish were the remains of a meal I hadn't given him. The stink of his rancid urine and warm shit contaminated everything. I had devoted myself to studying him in the way I studied Latin. The manual said that cats scratch at the ground to hide their droppings, and in houses without a courtyard, like this one, they would scratch in flower pots or some other hiding place. From the very first day it was advisable to provide them with a box of sand to redirect this habit, which I had done. It also said that the first thing they do in a new house is mark out their territory by urinating everywhere, which might be true, but the manual did not say how to prevent it. I followed his tracks to familiarize myself with his original habits, but I could not find his secret hiding places, his resting places, the causes of his erratic moods. I tried to teach him to eat on schedule, to use the litter box on the terrace, not to climb into my bed while I was sleeping or sniff at food on the table, and I could not make him understand that the house was his by his own right and not as the spoils of war. So I let him do whatever he wanted.

At dusk I faced the rainstorm, whose hurricane-force winds threatened to blow down the house. I suffered an attack of sneezing, my skull hurt, and I had a fever, but I felt possessed by a strength and determination I'd never had at any age or for any reason. I put pots on the floor under the leaks and realized that new ones had appeared since the previous winter. The largest had begun to flood the right side of the library. I hurried to rescue the Greek and Latin authors who lived there, but when I removed the books I discovered a stream spurting at high pressure from a broken pipe along the bottom of the wall. I did what I could to pack it with rags to give me time to save the books. The deafening noise of the rain and the howling of the wind intensified in the park. Then a phantasmal flash of lightning and a simultaneous clap of thunder saturated the air with a strong sulfur odor, the wind destroyed the balcony's window panes, and the awful sea squall broke the locks and came inside the house. And yet, in less than ten minutes, the sky cleared all at once. A splendid sun dried the streets filled with stranded trash, and the heat returned.

When the storm had passed I still had the feeling I was not alone in the house. My only explanation is that just as real events are forgotten, some that never were can be in our memories as if they had happened. For if I evoked the emergency of the rainstorm, I did not see myself alone in the house but always accompanied by Delgadina. I had felt her so close during the night that I detected the sound of her breath in the bedroom and the throbbing of her cheek on my pillow. It was the only way I could understand how we could have done so much in so short a time. I remembered standing on the library footstool and I remembered her awake in her little flowered dress taking the books from me to put them in a safe place. I saw her running from one end of the house to the other battling the storm, drenched with rain and in water up to her ankles. I remembered how the next day she prepared a breakfast that never was and set the table while I dried the floors and imposed order on the shipwreck of the house. I never forgot her somber look as we were eating: Why were you so old when we met? I answered with the truth: Age isn't how old you are but how old you feel.

From then on I had her in my memory with so much clarity that I could do what I wanted with her. I changed the color of her eyes according to my state of mind: the color of water when she woke, the color of syrup when she laughed, the color of light when she was annoyed. I dressed her according to the age and condition that suited my changes of mood: a novice in love at twenty, a parlor whore at forty, the queen of Babylon at seventy, a saint at one hundred. We sang Puccini love duets, Agustín Lara boleros, Carlos Gardel tangos, and we confirmed once again that those who do not sing cannot even imagine the joy of singing. Today I know it was not a hallucination but one more miracle of the first love of my life at the age of ninety.

When the house was in order I called Rosa Cabar-cas. Holy God! she exclaimed when she heard my voice, I thought you had drowned. She could not understand how I had spent another night with the girl and not touched her. You have the absolute right not to like her, but at least behave like an adult. I tried to explain, but with no transition she changed the subject: In any case, I have another one in mind for you who's a little older, beautiful, and also a virgin. Her father wants to trade her for a house, but we can discuss a discount. My heart froze. That's the last straw, I protested in horror, I want the same one, the way she always is, without failures, without fights, without bad memories. There was a silence on the line, and then the docile voice in which she said, as if talking to herself: Well, this must be what the doctors call senile dementia.

At ten that night I went there with a driver known for the unusual virtue of not asking questions. I took along a portable fan, a painting by Orlando Rivera—the beloved Figurita—and a hammer and nail to hang it on the wall. I stopped on the way to buy tooth-brushes, toothpaste, scented soap, Florida Water, and licorice lozenges. I also wanted to bring a nice vase and a bouquet of yellow roses to exorcise the inanity of paper flowers, but nothing was open and I had to steal a bouquet of newborn alstroemerias from a private garden.

On the instructions of the owner, from then on I arrived by the back street that ran along the aqueduct so no one would see me enter by the orchard gate. The driver warned me: Be careful, scholar, they kill in that house. I replied: If it's for love it doesn't matter. The courtyard was in darkness, but there were lights burning in the windows and a confusion of music playing in the six bedrooms. In mine, at top volume, I heard the warm voice of Don Pedro Vargas, the tenor of America, singing a bolero by Miguel Matamoros. I felt as if I were going to die. I pushed open the door, gasping for breath, and saw Delgadina in bed as she was in my memory: naked and sleeping in holy peace on the side of her heart.

Before I lay down I arranged the dressing table, replaced the rusty fan with the new one, and hung the picture where she could see it from the bed. I lay down beside her and examined her inch by inch. It was the same girl who had walked through my house: the same hands that recognized me by touch in the darkness, the same feet with their delicate step that became confused with the cat's, the same odor of sweat on my sheets, the same finger that wore the thimble. Incredible: seeing and touching her in the flesh, she seemed less real to me than in my memory.

There's a painting on the opposite wall, I told her. Figurita painted it, a man we loved very much, the best brothel dancer who ever lived, and so good-hearted he felt sorry for the devil. He painted it with ship's varnish on scorched canvas from a plane that crashed in the Sierra Nevada de Santa Marta, with brushes that he made with hair from his dog. The woman he painted is a nun he abducted from a convent and married. I'll leave it here so it will be the first thing you see when you wake up.

She hadn't changed position when I turned off the light, at one in the morning, and her respiration was so faint I took her pulse so I could feel she was alive. Blood circulated through her veins with the fluidity of a song that branched off into the most hidden areas of her body and returned to her heart, purified by love.

Before I left at dawn I drew the lines of her hand on a piece of paper and gave it to Diva Sahibí for a reading so I could know her soul. She said: A person who says only what she thinks. Perfect for manual labor. She's in contact with someone who has died and from whom she expects help, but she's mistaken: the help she's looking for is within reach of her hand. She's had no relationships, but she'll die an old woman, and married. Now she has a dark man, but he won't be the man of her life. She could have eight children but will decide for just three. At the age of thirty-five, if she does what her heart tells her and not her mind, she'll manage a lot of money, and at forty she'll receive an inheritance. She's going to travel a good deal. She has double life and double luck and can influence her own destiny. She likes to try everything, out of curiosity, but she'll be sorry if she isn't guided by her heart.

Tormented by love, I had the storm damage fixed and also took care of many other repairs I had put off for years because of insolvency or indolence. I reorganized the library according to the order in which I had read the books. And I discarded the player piano as a historical relic, along with more than a hundred rolls of classical music, and bought a used record player that was better than mine, with high-fidelity speakers that enlarged the area of the house. I was on the verge of ruin but well-compensated by the miracle of still being alive at my age.

The house rose from its ashes and I sailed on my love of Delgadina with an intensity and happiness I had never known in my former life. Thanks to her I confronted my inner self for the first time as my ninetieth year went by. I discovered that my obsession for having each thing in the right place, each subject at the right time, each word in the right style, was not the well-deserved reward of an ordered mind but just the opposite: a complete system of pretense invented by me to hide the disorder of my nature. I discovered that I am not disciplined out of virtue but as a reaction to my negligence, that I appear generous in order to conceal my meanness, that I pass myself off as prudent because I am evil-minded, that I am conciliatory in order not to succumb to my repressed rage, that I am punctual only to hide how little I care about other people's time. I learned, in short, that love is not a condition of the spirit but a sign of the zodiac.

I became another man. I tried to reread the classics that had guided me in adolescence, and I could not bear them. I buried myself in the romantic writings I had repudiated when my mother tried to impose them on me with a heavy hand, and in them I became aware that the invincible power that has moved the world is unrequited, not happy, love. When my tastes in music reached a crisis, I discovered that I was backward and old, and I opened my heart to the delights of chance.

I ask myself how I could give in to this perpetual vertigo that I in fact provoked and feared. I floated among erratic clouds and talked to myself in front of the mirror in the vain hope of confirming who I was. My delirium was so great that during a student demonstration complete with rocks and bottles, I had to make an enormous effort not to lead it as I held up a sign that would sanctify my truth: *I am mad with love*.

Disoriented by the merciless evocation of Delgadina asleep, with no malice at all I changed the spirit of my Sunday columns. Whatever the subject, I wrote them for her, laughed and cried over them for her, and my life poured into every word. Rather than the formula of a traditional personal column that they always had followed, I wrote them as love letters that all people could make their own. At the paper I proposed that instead of setting the text in linotype it be published in my Florentine handwriting. The editor in chief, of course, thought it was another attack of senile vanity, but the managing editor persuaded him with a phrase that is still making the rounds:

"Make no mistake: peaceful madmen are ahead of the future."

The response of the public was immediate and enthusiastic, with numerous letters from readers in love. Some columns were read on radio newscasts along with the latest crises, and mimeographs or carbon copies were made and sold like contraband cigarettes on the corners of Calle San Blas. From the start it was evident that the columns obeyed my longing to express myself, but I developed the habit of taking that into account when I wrote, always in the voice of a ninety-year-old who had not learned to think like an old man. The intellectual community, as usual, showed itself to be timid and divided, and even the most unexpected graphologists engaged in controversies regarding their inconsistent analyses of my handwriting. It was they who divided opinions, overheated the polemic, and made nostalgia popular.

Before the end of the year I had arranged with Rosa Cabarcas to leave in the room the electric fan, the toilet articles, and whatever else I might bring in the future to make it livable. I would arrive at ten, always with something new for her, or for both of us, and spend a few minutes taking out the hidden props to set up the theater of our nights. Before I left, never later than five, I would secure everything again under lock and key. Then the bedroom returned to its original squalor for the sad loves of casual clients. One morning I heard that Marcos Pérez, the most listened-to voice on radio after daybreak, had decided to read my Sunday columns on his Monday newscasts. When I could control my nausea I said in horror: Now you know, Delgadina, that fame is a very fat lady who doesn't sleep with you, but when you wake she's always at the foot of the bed, looking at us.

One day during this time I stayed to have breakfast with Rosa Cabarcas, who was beginning to seem less decrepit to me in spite of her rigorous mourning and the black bonnet that concealed her eyebrows. Her breakfasts were known to be splendid, and prepared with enough pepper to make me cry. At the first fiery bite I said, bathed in tears: Tonight I won't need a full moon for my asshole to burn. Don't complain, she said. If it burns it's because you still have one, thanks be to God.

She was surprised when I mentioned the name Delgadina. That isn't her name, she said, her name is . . . Don't tell me, I interrupted, for me she's Delgadina. She shrugged: All right, after all, she's yours, but to me it sounds like a diuretic. I mentioned the message about the tiger that the girl had written on the mirror. It couldn't have been her, Rosa said, she doesn't know how to read or write. Then who was it? She shrugged: It could be from somebody who died in the room.

I took advantage of those breakfasts to unburden myself to Rosa Cabarcas, and I requested small favors for the well-being and good appearance of Delgadina. She granted them without thinking about it, and with the mischievousness of a schoolgirl. How funny! she said at the time. I feel as if you were asking me for her hand. And speaking of that, she said in a casual way, why don't you marry her? I was dumbfounded. I'm serious, she insisted, it'll be cheaper. After all, at your age the problem is whether you can or can't, but you told me you have that problem solved. I cut her off: Sex is the consolation you have when you can't have love.

She burst into laughter. Ah, my scholar, I always knew you were a real man, you always were and I'm glad you still are while your enemies are surrendering their weapons. There's a reason they talk so much about you. Did you hear Marcos Pérez? Everybody hears him, I said, to change the subject. But she insisted: Professor Camacho y Cano, too, on *The*

Little Bit of Everything Hour, said yesterday that the world isn't what it once was because there aren't many men like you left.

That weekend I found that Delgadina had a fever and cough. I woke Rosa Cabarcas to ask for a household remedy, and she brought a first-aid kit to the room. Two days later Delgadina was still prostrate and had not been able to return to her routine of attaching buttons. The doctor had prescribed a household treatment for a common grippe that would be over in a week, but he was alarmed by her general malnourished state. I stopped seeing her, felt how much I missed her, and used the opportunity to arrange the room without her in it.

I also brought in a pen-and-ink drawing by Cecilia Porras for *We Were All Waiting*, Álvaro Cepeda's book of short stories. I brought the six volumes of Romain Rolland's *Jean Christophe* to help me through my wakeful nights. And so, when Delgadina was able to return to the room, she found it worthy of a sedentary happiness: the air purified by an aromatic insecticide, rose-colored walls, shaded lamps, fresh flowers in the vases, my favorite books, my mother's good paintings hung in a different way, according to modern tastes. I had replaced the old radio with a short-wave model that I kept tuned to a classical music program so that Delgadina would learn to sleep to Mozart's quartets, but one night I found it tuned to a station that specialized in popular boleros. It was her preference, no doubt, and I accepted this without sorrow, for I had cultivated the same preference in my better days. Before returning home the next day, I wrote on the mirror with her lipstick: *Dear girl, we are alone in the world.*

During this period I had the strange impression that she was growing older before her time. I mentioned this to Rosa Cabarcas, who thought it was natural. She turns fifteen on December 5, she said. A perfect Sagittarius. It troubled me that she was real enough to have birthdays. What could I give her? A bicycle, said Rosa Cabarcas. She has to cross the city twice a day to sew on buttons. In the back room she showed me the bicycle Delgadina used, and the truth was it seemed a piece of junk unworthy of so well-loved a woman. Still, it moved me as a tangible proof that Delgadina existed in real life.

When I went to buy her the best bicycle, I couldn't resist the temptation of trying it, and I rode it a few casual times along the ramp in the store. When the salesman asked me how old I was, I responded with the coquetry of age: I'm almost ninety-one. He said just what I wanted him to: Well, you look twenty years younger. I didn't understand myself how I had retained that schoolboy's skill, and I felt myself over-flowing with a radiant joy. I began to sing. First to myself, in a quiet voice, and then at full volume, with the airs of the great Caruso, in the midst of the public market's garish shops and demented traffic. People looked at me in amusement, called to me, urged me to participate in the Vuelta a Colombia bicycle race in a wheelchair. I responded with the salute of a happy mariner, not interrupting my song. That week, in tribute to December, I wrote another bold column: "How to Be Happy on a Bicycle at the Age of Ninety."

On the night of her birthday I sang the entire song to Delgadina, and I kissed her all over her body until I was breathless: her spine, vertebra by vertebra, down to her languid buttocks, the side with the mole, the side of her inexhaustible heart. As I kissed her the heat of her body increased, and it exhaled a wild, untamed fragrance. She responded with new vibrations along every inch of her skin, and on each one I found a distinctive heat, a unique taste, a different moan, and her entire body resonated inside with an arpeggio, and her nipples opened and flowered without being touched. I was beginning to fall asleep in the small hours when I heard something like the sound of multitudes in the sea and a panic in the trees that pierced my heart. I went to the bathroom and wrote on the mirror: *Delgadina, my love, the Christmas breezes have arrived.*

One of my happiest memories was a disturbance I felt on a similar morning as I was leaving school. What's wrong with me? The dazed teacher said: Ah, my boy, can't you see it's the breezes? Eighty years later I felt it again when I woke in Delgadina's bed, and it was the same punctual December returning with its translucent skies, its sandstorms, its whirlwinds in the streets that blew the roofs off houses and lifted the skirts of schoolgirls. This was when the city acquired a spectral resonance. On breezy nights, even in the neighborhoods in the hills, shouts from the public market could be heard as if they were just around the corner. It was not unusual for the December gusts to allow us to locate friends, scattered among distant brothels, by the sound of their voices.

The breezes, however, also brought me the bad news that Delgadina could not spend the Christmas holidays with me but would be with her family. If I

detest anything in this world it is the obligatory cele-
brations with people crying because they're happy,
artificial fires, inane carols, crepe-paper wreaths that
have nothing to do with the child born two thousand
years ago in a poor stable. Still, when night came I
could not resist my nostalgia and I went to the room
without her. I slept well and woke next to a plush bear
that walked on its hind legs like a polar bear, and a
card that said: *For the ugly papá*. Rosa Cabarcas had
told me that Delgadina was learning to read from the
lessons I wrote on the mirror, and I thought her nice
handwriting admirable. But the owner punctured my
illusions with the awful news that the bear was her
gift, and therefore on New Year's Eve I stayed home
and was in bed by eight, and fell asleep without bit-
terness. I was happy, because at the stroke of twelve,
in the midst of the furious pealing of the bells, the
factory and fire-engine sirens, the lamentations of
ships, the explosion of fireworks and rockets, I sensed
that Delgadina tiptoed in, lay down beside me, and
gave me a kiss. So real that her licorice scent remained
on my mouth.

4

A T THE BEGINNING of the new year we started
to know each other as well as if we lived
together awake, for I had discovered a cautious tone
of voice that she heard without waking, and she
would answer me with the natural language of her
body. Her states of mind could be seen in the way
she slept. Exhausted and unpolished at first, she was
approaching an inner peace that beautified her face
and enriched her sleep. I told her about my life, I read
into her ear the first drafts of my Sunday columns in
which, without my saying so, she and she alone was
present.

During this time I left on her pillow a pair of emer-
ald earrings that had belonged to my mother. She

wore them to our next rendezvous but they didn't look good on her. Then I brought a pair better suited to her skin color. I explained: The first ones I brought weren't right for your type and your haircut. These will look better. She didn't wear any earrings at all to our next two meetings, but for the third she put on the ones I had suggested. In this way I began to understand that she did not obey my orders but waited for an opportunity to please me. By now I felt so accustomed to this kind of domestic life that I no longer slept naked but wore the Chinese silk pajamas I had stopped using because I hadn't had anyone to take them off for.

I began to read her *The Little Prince* by Saint-Exupéry, a French author whom the entire world admires more than the French do. It was the first book to entertain her without waking her, and in fact I had to go there two days in a row to finish reading it to her. We continued with Perrault's *Tales*, *Sacred History*, the *Arabian Nights* in a version sanitized for children, and because of the differences among them I realized that her sleep had various levels of profundity depending on her interest in the readings. When I sensed she had touched the deepest level I turned out the light and slept with my arms around her until the roosters crowed.

I felt so happy that I would kiss her eyelids with very gentle kisses, and one night it happened like a light in the sky: she smiled for the first time. Later, for no reason at all, she rolled over in bed, turned her back to me, and said in vexation: It was Isabel who made the snails cry. Excited by the hope of a dialogue, I asked in the same tone: Whose were they? She didn't answer. Her voice had a plebeian touch, as if it belonged not to her but to someone else she carried inside. That was when the last shadow of a doubt disappeared from my soul: I preferred her asleep.

My only problem was the cat. He would not eat and was unsociable and spent two days in his habitual corner without raising his head, and he clawed at me like a wounded beast when I tried to put him in the wicker basket so that Damiana could take him to the veterinarian. It was all she could do to control him, and she carried him there, protesting, in a burlap sack. In a while she called from the shelter to say that he had to be put down and they needed my authorization. Why? Because he's very old, said Damiana. I thought in a rage that they could also roast me alive in an oven filled with cats. I felt caught between two fires: I had not learned to love the cat, but neither did I have the heart to order him killed just because he was old. Where did the manual say that?

The incident disturbed me so much that I wrote the Sunday column with a title usurped from Neruda: "Is the Cat a Minuscule Salon Tiger?" The column gave rise to a new campaign that once again divided readers into those who were for and those who were against cats. After five days the prevailing thesis was that it might be legitimate to put down a cat for reasons of public health but not because it was old.

After the death of my mother, I would be kept awake by my terror that someone might touch me while I was sleeping. One night I felt her touch, but her voice restored my serenity: *Figlio mio poveretto*. I felt the same thing late one night in Delgadina's room, and I twisted with delight, believing she had touched me. But no: it was Rosa Cabarcas in the dark. Get dressed and come with me, she said, I have a serious problem.

She did, and it was more serious than I could have imagined. One of the house's important clients had been stabbed to death in the first room in the pavilion. The killer had escaped. The enormous corpse, naked but with shoes on, had the pallor of steamed chicken in the blood-soaked bed. I recognized him as soon as I walked in: it was J.M.B., an important banker, famous for his elegant bearing, his good nature, his fine clothes, and above all for the smartness of his home. On his neck he had two purple wounds like lips, and a gash on his belly was still bleeding. Rigor had not yet set in. More than his wounds, what struck me was that he wore a condom, to all appearances unused, on his sex that was shrunken by death.

Rosa Cabarcas did not know whom he had been with because he too had the privilege of coming in by the orchard entrance. The suspicion was not discounted that his companion might have been another man. The only thing the owner wanted from me was help in dressing the body. She was so steady that I was disturbed by the idea that, for her, death was a mere kitchen matter. There's nothing more difficult than dressing a dead man, I said. I've done it more than once, she replied. It's easy if somebody holds him for me. I pointed out: Who do you imagine is going to believe that a body sliced up by stab wounds is inside the undamaged clothes of an English gentleman?

I trembled for Delgadina. The best thing would be

for you to take her with you, said Rosa Cabarcas. I'd rather die first, I said, my saliva icy. She saw this and could not hide her disdain: You're trembling! For her, I said, though it was only half true. Tell her to leave before anybody comes. All right, she said, though as a reporter nothing will happen to you. Or to you either, I said with a certain rancor. You're the only liberal with power in this government.

The city, so sought-after for its peaceful nature and congenital safety, was degraded by the misfortune of a scandalous, brutal murder every year. This one wasn't it. The official news report, with headlines that were too big and details that were too scant, said the young banker had been attacked and stabbed to death for unknown reasons on the Pradomar highway. He had no enemies. The government communiqué indicated that the presumed killers were refugees from the interior of the country who were unleashing a crime wave foreign to the civic spirit of the city's residents. In the first few hours more than fifty arrests were made.

Scandalized, I turned to the legal reporter, a typical newspaperman from the twenties who wore a green eyeshade and elastic bands on his sleeves and took pride in anticipating the facts. He, however, knew only a few stray threads of the crime, and I filled him in as much as prudence would allow. And so with four hands we wrote five pages of copy for an eight-column article on the front page, attributed to the eternal phantom of reliable sources in whom we had complete confidence. But the Abominable No-Man—the censor—did not hesitate to impose the official version that it had been an attack by liberal outlaws. I purified my conscience with a scowl of mourning at the most cynical and well-attended funeral of the century.

When I returned home that night I called Rosa Cabarcas to find out what had happened to Delgadina, but she did not answer the phone for four days. On the fifth I went to her house with clenched teeth. The doors were sealed, not by the police but by the health department. Nobody in the area knew anything about anything. With no sign of Delgadina, I began a furious and at times ridiculous search that left me gasping for breath. I spent entire days observing young female cyclists from the benches in a dusty park where children at play climbed to the top of the peeling statue of Simón Bolívar. They pedaled past like doe: beautiful, available, ready to be caught in a game of blindman's bluff. When I had no more hope I took refuge in the peace of boleros. That was like a lethal potion: every word was Delgadina. I always had needed silence to write because my mind would pay more attention to the music than to my writing. Now it was the reverse: I could write only in the shade of boleros. My life became filled with her. The columns I wrote during those two weeks were models in code for love letters. The managing editor, annoyed by the avalanche of responses, asked me to moderate the love while we thought of a way to console so many lovelorn readers.

The lack of serenity put an end to the precision of my days. I woke at five but stayed in the darkened room imagining Delgadina in her unreal life as she woke her brothers and sisters, dressed them for school, gave them breakfast if there was any food, and bicycled across the city to serve out her sentence of sewing buttons. I asked myself in astonishment: What does a woman think about while she attaches a button? Did she think of me? Was she also looking for Rosa Cabarcas to find out about me? For a week I did not take off my mechanic's coverall day or night,

I did not bathe or shave or brush my teeth, because love taught me too late that you groom yourself for someone, you dress and perfume yourself for someone, and I'd never had anyone to do that for. Damiana thought I was sick when she found me naked in the hammock at ten in the morning. I looked at her with eyes clouded by desire and invited her to a naked roll in the hay. She, with some scorn, said:

"Have you thought about what you'll do if I say yes?"

In this way I learned how much my suffering had corrupted me. I did not recognize myself in my adolescent's pain. I did not go out, so as not to leave the phone unattended. I wrote without taking it off the hook, and at the first ring I would rush to answer it, thinking it might be Rosa Cabarcas. I kept interrupting whatever I was doing to call her, and I repeated this for days on end until I realized it was a phone without a heart.

When I returned home one rainy afternoon I found the cat curled up on the front steps. He was dirty, battered, and so meek it filled me with compassion. The manual informed me he was sick, and I followed its rules for making him feel better. Then, all at once, while I was having a siesta, I was awakened by the idea that he could lead me to Delgadina's house. I carried him in a shopping bag to Rosa Cabarcas's shop, still sealed and showing no signs of life, but he twisted around so much in the bag that he managed to escape, jumped over the orchard wall, and disappeared among the trees. I banged on the door with my fist, and a military voice asked without opening it: Who goes there? A friend, I said, not to be outdone. I'm looking for the owner. There is no owner, said the voice. At least open up so I can get my cat, I insisted. There is no cat, it said. I asked: Who are you?

"Nobody," said the voice.

I always had understood that dying of love was mere poetic license. That afternoon, back home again without the cat and without her, I proved that it was not only possible but that I myself, an old man without anyone, was dying of love. But I also realized that the contrary was true as well: I would not have traded the delights of my suffering for anything in the world. I had spent more than fifteen years trying to translate the poems of Leopardi, and only on that afternoon did I have a profound sense of them: *Ah, me, if this is love, then how it torments.*

My going to the paper in a coverall and unshaven awoke certain doubts regarding my mental state. The remodeled offices, with individual glass cubicles and skylights, looked like a maternity hospital. The artificial climate, silent and comfortable, invited speaking in whispers and walking on tiptoe. In the lobby, like dead viceroys, were oil portraits of the three editors-for-life and photographs of illustrious visitors. The enormous main room was presided over by the gigantic photograph of the current editorial staff taken on the afternoon of my birthday. I could not avoid a mental comparison to the one taken when I was thirty, and once again I confirmed with horror that one ages more and with more intensity in pictures than in reality. The secretary who had kissed me on the afternoon of my birthday asked if I was sick. I was happy to respond with the truth so she would not believe it: Sick with love. She said: Too bad it's not for me! I returned the compliment: Don't be so sure.

The legal reporter came out of his cubicle shouting that two bodies of unidentified girls were in the city morgue. Frightened, I asked him: What age? Young, he said. They may be refugees from the interior chased here by the regime's thugs. I sighed with relief. The situation encroaches on us in silence, like a bloodstain, I said. The legal reporter, at some distance now, shouted:

"Not blood, Maestro, shit."

Something worse happened to me a few days later, when a fast-moving girl carrying a basket the same as the cat's passed like a shudder in front of the Mundo Bookstore. I followed her, elbowing my way through the crowd in the clamor of noon. She was very beautiful, with long strides and a fluidity in finding her way past people that made it difficult for me to catch up to her. At last I passed her and looked into her face. She moved me aside with her hand, not stopping and not begging my pardon. She was not who I had thought, but her haughtiness wounded me as if she were. I understood then that I would not be able to recognize Delgadina awake and dressed, nor could she know me if she had never seen me. In an act of madness, I crocheted twelve pairs of blue and pink infant's booties in three days, trying to give myself the courage not to hear or sing or think about the songs that reminded me of her.

The truth was that I could not manage my soul, and I was becoming aware of old age because of my weakness in the face of love. I had even more dramatic proof of this when a public bus ran down a girl on a bicycle in the middle of the business district. She had just been taken away in an ambulance, and the magnitude of the tragedy could be seen in the scrap metal that the bicycle, lying in a pool of bright blood, had been reduced to. But I was affected not so much by the ruined bicycle as by the brand, model, and color. It had to be the one I had given Delgadina.

The witnesses agreed that the injured cyclist was very young, tall and slim, with short curly hair. Stunned, I hailed the first taxi I saw and took it to the Hospital de Caridad, an old building with ocher walls that looked like a prison bogged down in quicksand. It took me half an hour to get in and another half hour to get out of a courtyard fragrant with fruit trees where a woman in distress blocked my way, looked into my eyes, and exclaimed:

"I'm the one you're not looking for."

Only then did I remember that this was where nonviolent patients from the municipal asylum lived without restraints. I had to identify myself as a reporter to hospital management before a nurse would take me to the emergency ward. The information was in the admissions book: Rosalba Ríos, sixteen, no known employment. Diagnosis: cerebral concussion. Prognosis: guarded. I asked the head of the ward if I could see her, hoping in my heart that he would say no, but I was taken to her, for they were delighted by the idea that I might want to write about the neglected state of the hospital.

We crossed a cluttered ward that had a strong smell of carbolic acid, and patients crowded into the beds. At the rear, in a single room, lying on a metal cot, was the girl we were looking for. Her skull was covered with bandages, her face indecipherable, swollen, and black-and-blue, but all I needed to see were her feet to know she wasn't Delgadina. Only then did it occur to me to wonder: What would I have done if it had been?

Still entangled in the night's cobwebs, the next day I found the courage to go to the shirt factory where Rosa Cabarcas had once told me the girl worked, and I asked the owner to show us his plant as a model for a continent-wide project of the United Nations. He was an elephantine, taciturn Lebanese who opened the doors to his kingdom in the illusory hope of being an example to the world.

Three hundred girls in white blouses with Ash Wednesday crosses on their foreheads were sewing buttons in the vast, illuminated nave. When they saw us come in they sat up straight, like schoolgirls, and watched out of the corners of their eyes as the manager explained his contributions to the immemorial art of attaching buttons. I scrutinized each of their faces, terrified that I would discover Delgadina dressed and awake. But it was one of them who discovered me with a frightening look of pitiless admiration:

"Tell me, Señor, aren't you the man who writes love letters in the paper?"

I never would have imagined that a sleeping girl could cause so much devastation in me. I escaped the factory without saying goodbye or even wondering if one of those virgins in purgatory was at last the one I was seeking. When I walked out, the only feeling I had left in life was the desire to cry.

Rosa Cabarcas called after a month with an incredible explanation: following the banker's murder, she had taken a well-deserved rest in Cartagena de Indias. I didn't believe her, of course, but I congratulated her on her good luck and allowed her to expatiate on her lie before asking the question boiling in my heart:

"What about her?"

Rosa Cabarcas fell silent for a long time. She's there, she said at last, but her voice became evasive:

You have to wait a while. How long? I have no idea, I'll let you know. I felt she was getting away from me and I stopped her cold: Wait, you have to shed some light on this. There is no light, she said, and concluded: Be careful, you can do yourself harm and, above all, you can do her harm. I was in no mood for that kind of coyness. I pleaded for at least a chance to approach the truth. After all, I said, we're accomplices. She didn't take another step. Calm down, she said, the girl's all right and waiting for me to call her, but right now there's nothing to do and I'm not saying anything else. Goodbye.

I was left holding the telephone, not knowing how to proceed, because I also knew her well enough to think I wouldn't get anything from her unless she chose to give it. Later in the afternoon I made a furtive visit to her house, trusting more to chance than to reason, and I found it still locked, sealed by the health department. I thought Rosa Cabarcas had called from somewhere else, perhaps from another city, and the mere idea filled me with dark presentiments. But at six that evening, when I least expected it, she pronounced my own password on the telephone:

"All right, today's the day."

At ten that night, tremulous and biting my lips to

keep from crying, I arrived carrying boxes of Swiss chocolates, nougat, and candies, and a basket of fiery roses to cover the bed. The door was half-open, the lights turned on, and Brahms's First Sonata for Violin and Piano was being diluted at half volume on the radio. In the bed, Delgadina looked so radiant and so different that it was hard for me to recognize her.

She had grown, but you could see this not in her stature but in an intense maturity that made her seem two or three years older, and more naked than ever. Her high cheekbones, her skin tanned by the suns of rough seas, her delicate lips, and her short curly hair imbued her face with the androgynous splendor of Praxiteles' *Apollo*. But no equivocation was possible, because her breasts had grown so much they didn't fit in my hand, her hips had finished developing, and her bones had become firmer and more harmonious. I was charmed by these achievements of nature but stunned by the artifice: false eyelashes, mother-of-pearl polish on the nails of her fingers and toes, and a cheap perfume that had nothing to do with love. Still, what drove me mad was the fortune she was wearing: gold earrings with clusters of emeralds, a necklace of natural pearls, a gold bracelet gleaming with diamonds, and rings with legitimate stones on every finger. On the chair was her evening dress covered with sequins and embroidery, and satin slippers. A strange vertigo rose from deep inside me.

"Whore!" I shouted.

For the devil breathed a sinister thought into my ear. And that was: on the night of the crime, Rosa Cabarcas could not have had the time or composure to warn the girl, and the police found her in the room, alone, a minor, with no alibi. Nobody like Rosa Cabarcas in a situation like that: she sold the girl's virginity to one of her big-shot clients in exchange for being cleared of the crime. The first thing, of course, was to disappear until the scandal died down. How marvelous! A honeymoon for three, the two of them in bed, and Rosa Cabarcas on a deluxe terrace enjoying her happy impunity. Blind with senseless fury, I began smashing everything in the room against the wall: lamps, radio, fan, mirrors, pitchers, glasses. I did it without haste but also without pause, with great crashes and a methodical intoxication that saved my life. The girl gave a start at the first explosion of noise but did not look at me; instead, she turned her back and remained that way, showing intermittent spasms, until the crashing ended. The chickens in the courtyard and the late-night dogs added to the uproar.

With the blinding lucidity of rage I had a final inspiration to set fire to the house when the impassive figure of Rosa Cabarcas, dressed in a nightgown, appeared in the door. She said nothing. She made a visual inventory of the disaster and confirmed that the girl was curled up like a snail, her head hidden between her arms: terrified but intact.

"My God!" Rosa Cabarcas exclaimed. "What I wouldn't have given for a love like this!"

She looked at me from head to toe with a compassionate glance and commanded: Let's go. I followed her to the house, she poured me a glass of water in silence, gestured for me to sit down across from her, and prepared to hear my confession. All right, she said, now behave like an adult and tell me what's wrong.

I told her what I considered my revealed truth. Rosa Cabarcas listened to me in silence, without surprise, and at last she seemed enlightened. How wonderful, she said. I've always said that jealousy knows more than truth does. And then, without reticence, she told me the reality. In effect, she said, in her confusion on the night of the crime she had forgotten about the girl sleeping in the room. One of her clients, who was also the dead man's lawyer, distributed benefits and bribes with a free hand and invited Rosa Cabarcas to stay at a quiet hotel in Cartagena de Indias until the scandal died down. Believe me, said Rosa Cabarcas, in all this time I never stopped thinking about you and the girl. I came back the day before yesterday and the first thing I did was call you, but there was no answer. On the other hand, the girl came right away, in such bad shape that I bathed her for you, dressed her for you, sent her to the hairdresser for you, and told them to make her as pretty as a queen. You saw how she looked: perfect. Her luxury clothes? One of the dresses I rent to my poorest girls when they have to go dancing with their clients. The jewels? They're mine, she said: All you have to do is touch them to see that the stones are glass and the precious metals tin. So stop fucking around, she concluded: Go on, wake her, beg her pardon, and take charge of her once and for all. Nobody deserves to be happier than you two.

I made a superhuman effort to believe her, but love was stronger than reason. Whores! I said, tormented by the living flame burning in my belly. That's what you are! I shouted: Damned whores! I don't want to know any more about you, or about any other slut in this world, least of all her. From the door I made a gesture: goodbye forever. Rosa Cabarcas did not doubt it.

"Go with God," she said, grimacing with sorrow, and she returned to her real life. "Anyway, I'll send you a bill for the mess you made in my room."

5

As I was reading *The Ides of March*, I ran across an ominous sentence that the author attributes to Julius Caesar: *In the end, it is impossible not to become what others believe you are*. I could not confirm its real origin in the writing of Julius Caesar himself or in the works of his biographers, from Suetonius to Carcopinus, but it was worth knowing. Its fatalism, applied to the course of my life in the months that followed, gave me the determination I needed not only to write these memories but to begin them without diffidence, with the love of Delgadina.

I did not have a moment's peace, I almost stopped eating, and I lost so much weight my trousers were loose around my waist. I had erratic pains in my bones, my mood would change for no reason, I spent my nights in a dazzled state that did not allow me to read or listen to music, while I wasted the days nodding in a stupefied somnolence that did not lead to sleep.

Relief came from out of the blue. On the crowded Loma Fresca bus, a woman sitting next to me, whom I didn't see get on, whispered in my ear: Are you still fucking? It was Casilda Armenta, an old love-for-hire who had put up with me as an assiduous client from the time she was a haughty adolescent. When she retired, ailing and without a cent, she married a Chinese vegetable farmer who gave her his name and support, and perhaps a little love. At the age of seventy-three she weighed what she always had, was still beautiful, had a strong character, and maintained intact the audacious speech of her trade.

She took me to her house, on a farm of Chinese laborers on a hill along the highway to the ocean. We sat on beach chairs on the shaded terrace, surrounded by ferns and the foliage of alstroemerias, and birdcages hanging from the eaves. On the side of the hill one could see the Chinese farmers in cone-shaped hats planting vegetables in the blazing sun, and the gray waters of the Bocas de Ceniza with the two dikes made of rocks that channel the river for several leagues into the sea. As we talked we saw a white ocean liner enter the outlet, and we followed it in silence until we heard its doleful bull's bellow at the river port. She sighed. Do you know something? In more than half a century, this is the first time I haven't received you in bed. We're not who we were, I said. She continued without hearing me: Every time they say things about you on the radio, applaud you for the affection people feel for you, call you the maestro of love, just imagine, I think that nobody knew your charms and your manias as well as I did. I'm serious, she said, nobody could have put up with you better.

I could not bear it any more. She sensed it, saw my eyes wet with tears, and only then must have discovered I was no longer the man I had been, and I endured her glance with a courage I never thought I had. The truth is I'm getting old, I said. We already are old, she said with a sigh. What happens is that you don't feel it on the inside, but from the outside everybody can see it.

It was impossible not to open my heart to her, and so I told her the complete story burning deep inside me, from my first call to Rosa Cabarcas on the eve of my ninetieth birthday to the tragic night when I smashed up the room and never went back. She listened to me unburden myself as if she were living through it herself, pondered it without haste, and at last she smiled.

"Do whatever you want, but don't lose that child," she said. "There's no greater misfortune than dying alone."

We went to Puerto Colombia in the little toy train as slow as a horse. We had lunch across from the worm-eaten wooden dock where everyone had entered the country before the Bocas de Ceniza was dredged. We sat under a roof of palm where large black matrons served fried red snapper with coconut rice and slices of green plantain. We dozed in the dense torpor of two o'clock and continued talking until the immense fiery sun sank into the ocean. Reality seemed fantastic to me. Look where our honeymoon has ended up, she mocked. But then she was serious: Today I look back, I see the line of thousands of men who passed through my beds, and I'd give my soul to have stayed with even the worst of them. Thank God I found my Chinaman in time. It's like being married to your little finger, but he's all mine.

She looked into my eyes, gauged my reaction to what she had just told me, and said: So you go and find that poor creature right now even if what your jealousy tells you is true, no matter what, nobody can take away the dances you've already had. But one thing, no grandfather's romanticism. Wake her, fuck her brains out with that burro's cock the devil gave you as a reward for cowardice and stinginess. I'm serious, she concluded, speaking from the heart: Don't let yourself die without knowing the wonder of fucking with love.

My hand trembled the next day when I dialed the number, as much because of the tension of my reunion with Delgadina as my uncertainty as to how Rosa Cabarcas would respond. We'd had a serious dispute over her abusive billing for the damage I'd done to her room. I had to sell one of the paintings most loved by my mother, estimated to be worth a fortune but at the moment of truth not amounting to a tenth of what I had hoped for. I increased that amount with the rest of my savings and took the money to Rosa Cabarcas with an unappealable ultimatum: Take it or leave it. It was a suicidal act, because if she had sold just one of my secrets she could have destroyed my good name. She did not dig in her heels, but she kept the paintings she had taken as security on the night of our argument. I was the absolute loser in a single play: I was left without Delgadina, without Rosa Cabarcas, and without the last of my savings. However, I listened to the phone ring once, twice, three times, and at last she said: Yes? My voice failed me. I hung up. I lay down in the hammock, trying to restore my serenity with the ascetic lyricism of Satie, and I perspired so much the canvas was soaked through. I did not have the courage to call again until the next day.

"All right, woman," I said in a firm voice. "Today's the day."

Rosa Cabarcas, of course, was above everything. Ah, my sad scholar, and she sighed with her invincible spirit, you disappear for two months and only come back to ask for illusions. She told me she hadn't seen Delgadina for more than a month, that the girl seemed to have recovered so well from her fright at my destructiveness that she didn't even mention it or ask for me, and was very happy in a new job, more comfortable and better-paid than sewing on buttons. A wave of living fire burned me inside. She can only be working as a whore, I said. Rosa replied without batting an eye: Don't be stupid, if that were true she'd be here. Where would she be better off? The rapidity of her logic made my doubts worse: And how do I know she isn't there? If she is, she replied, it's better for you not to know. Isn't that right? Once again I hated her. She was impervious and promised to track her down. Without much hope, because the neighbor's telephone where she used to call her had been turned off and she had no idea where the girl lived. But that was no reason to die, what the hell, she said, I'll call you in an hour.

It was an hour that lasted three days, but she found the girl available and healthy. I returned, mortified, and kissed every inch of her, as penitence, from twelve that night until the roosters crowed. A long forgive-me that I promised myself I would continue to repeat forever, and it was like starting again from the beginning. The room had been dismantled, and hard usage had done away with everything I had put in it. Rosa Cabarcas had left it that way and said I would have to take care of any improvements as payment for what I still owed her. My economic situation, however, had touched bottom. The money from my pensions covered less and less. The few salable items left in the house—except for my mother's sacred jewels—lacked commercial value, and nothing was old enough to be an antique. In better days, the governor had made me a tempting offer to buy en bloc the books of Greek, Latin, and Spanish classics for the Departmental Library, but I didn't have the heart to sell them. Later, given political changes and the deterioration of the world, nobody in the government thought about either arts or letters. Weary of searching for a decent solution, I put the jewels that Delgadina had returned to me in my pocket and went to pawn them in a sinister alley that led to the public market. With the air of a distracted scholar I walked back and forth along that hellhole crowded with shabby taverns, secondhand bookstores, and pawnshops, but the dignity of Florina de Dios blocked my way: I did not dare. Then I decided to sell them with head held high at the oldest and most reputable jewelry store.

The salesman asked me a few questions as he examined the jewels with his loupe. He had the awe-inspiring demeanor and style of a physician. I explained that they were jewels inherited from my mother. He acknowledged each of my explanations with a grunt, and at last he removed the loupe.

"I'm sorry," he said, "but they're the bottoms of bottles."

Seeing my surprise, he explained with gentle commiseration: Just as well that the gold is gold and the platinum platinum. I touched my pocket to make certain I had brought the purchase receipts, and without querulousness I said:

"Well, they were purchased in this noble house more than one hundred years ago."

His expression did not change. It tends to happen, he said, that in inherited jewels the most valuable stones keep disappearing over time, replaced by wayward members of the family or criminal jewelers, and only when someone tries to sell them is the fraud discovered. But give me a second, he said, and he took the jewels and went through a door in the rear. After a moment he returned, and with no explanation indicated that I should take a seat, and he continued working.

I examined the shop. I had gone there several times with my mother, and I remembered a recurring phrase: *Don't tell your papá*. All at once I had an idea that put me on edge: wasn't it possible that Rosa Cabarcas and Delgadina, by mutual agreement, had sold the legitimate stones and returned the jewels to me with fake ones?

I was burning with doubts when a secretary asked me to follow her through the same door in the rear, into a small office with long bookshelves that held thick volumes. A colossal Bedouin at a desk on the far side of the office stood and shook my hand, calling me *tú* with the effusiveness of an old friend. We were in secondary school together, he said by way of greeting. It was easy to remember him: he was the best soccer player in the school and the champion in our first brothels. I had lost track of him at some point, and I must have looked so decrepit to him that he confused me with a classmate from his childhood.

Lying open on the glass top of the desk was one of the hefty tomes from the archive that contained the memory of my mother's jewelry. A precise account, with dates and details of how she in person had changed the stones of two generations of beautiful and worthy Cargamantos, and had sold the legitimate ones to this same store. It had occurred when the father of the current owner was at the front of the jewelry store and he and I were in school. But he reassured me: these little tricks were common practice among great families in difficult times to resolve financial emergencies without sacrificing honor. Faced with crude reality, I preferred to keep them as a memento of another Florina de Dios whom I never had known.

Early in July I felt my true distance from death. My heart skipped beats and I began to see and feel all around me unmistakable presentiments of the end. The clearest occurred at a Bellas Artes concert. The air-conditioning had broken down, and the elite of arts and letters was cooking in a bain-marie in the crowded hall, but the magic of the music created a celestial climate. At the end, with the Allegretto poco mosso, I was shaken by the stunning revelation that I was listening to the last concert fate would afford me before I died. I did not feel sorrow or fear but an overwhelming emotion at having lived long enough to experience it.

When at last, drenched with perspiration, I managed to make my way past embraces and photographs, to my surprise I ran into Ximena Ortiz, like a hundred-year-old goddess in her wheelchair. Her mere presence imposed its burden on me like a mortal sin. She had a tunic of ivory-colored silk as smooth as her skin, a three-loop strand of real pearls, hair the color of mother-of-pearl cut in the style of the 1920s, with the tip of a gull's wing on her cheek, and large yellow eyes illuminated by the natural shadow of dark circles. Everything about her contradicted the rumor that her mind was becoming a blank through an unredeemable erosion of her memory. Petrified and in front of her without resources, I overcame the fiery vapor that rose to my face and greeted her in silence with a Versaillesque bow. She smiled like a queen and grasped my hand. Then I realized that this too was one of fate's vindications, and I did not lose the opportunity to pull out a thorn that had bothered me for so long. I've dreamed of this moment for years, I said. She did not seem to understand. You don't say! she said. And who are you? I never knew if in fact she had forgotten or if it was the final revenge of her life.

The certainty of being mortal, on the other hand, had taken me by surprise a short while before my fiftieth birthday on a similar occasion, a night during carnival when I danced an apache tango with a phenomenal woman whose face I never saw, heavier than me by forty pounds and taller by about a foot, yet who let herself be led like a feather in the wind. We danced so close together I could feel her blood circulating through her veins, and I was lulled by pleasure at her hard breathing, her ammoniac odor, her astronomical breasts, when I was shaken for the first time and almost knocked to the ground by the roar of death. It was like a brutal oracle in my ear: No matter what you do, this year or in the next hundred, you will be dead forever. She pulled away in fright: What's the matter? Nothing, I said, trying to control my heart:

"I'm trembling because of you."

From then on I began to measure my life not by years but by decades. The decade of my fifties had been decisive because I became aware that almost everybody was younger than I. The decade of my sixties was the most intense because of the suspicion that I no longer had the time to make mistakes. My seventies were frightening because of a certain possibility that the decade might be the last. Still, when I woke alive on the first morning of my nineties in the happy bed of Delgadina, I was transfixed by the agreeable idea that life was not something that passes by like Heraclitus' ever-changing river but a unique opportunity to turn over on the grill and keep broiling on the other side for another ninety years.

I became a man of easy tears. Any emotion that had anything to do with tenderness brought a lump to my throat that I could not always control, and I thought about renouncing the solitary pleasure of watching over Delgadina's sleep, less for the uncertainty of my death than for the sorrow of imagining her without me for the rest of her life. On one of those uncertain days, I happened to find myself on the very noble Calle de los Notarios, and I was surprised to discover nothing more than the rubble of the cheap old hotel where I had been initiated by force into the arts of love a short while before my twelfth birthday. It had been the mansion of shipbuilders, splendid like few others in the city, with columns overlaid in alabaster and gilded friezes around an interior courtyard and a glass cupola in seven colors that shone with the brilliance of a conservatory. For more than a century, on the ground floor with its gothic door to the street, the colonial notary's offices had been located where my father worked, prospered, and was ruined throughout a lifetime of fantastic dreams. Little by little the historic families abandoned the upper floors, which came to be occupied by a legion of ladies of the night in straitened circumstances who went up and down the stairs until dawn with clients caught for a peso and a half in the taverns of the nearby river port.

I was almost twelve, still wearing short pants and my elementary-school boots, and I could not resist the temptation of seeing the upper floors while my father debated in one of his interminable meetings, and I encountered a celestial sight. The women who sold their bodies at bargain prices until dawn moved around the house after eleven in the morning, when the heat from the stained glass became unbearable, and they were obliged to live their domestic life walking naked through the house while they shouted observations on the night's adventures. I was terrified. The only thing I could think of was to escape the way I had come in, when one of the naked women whose solid flesh was fragrant with rustic soap embraced me from behind and carried me to her pasteboard cubicle without my being able to see her, in the midst of shouts and applause from the bareskinned residents. She threw me face-up on her bed for four, removed my trousers in a masterful maneuver, and straddled me, but the icy terror that drenched my body kept me from receiving her like a man. That night, sleepless in my bed at home because of the shame of the assault, my longing to see her again would not allow me to sleep more than an hour. But the next morning, while night owls slept, I climbed trembling to her cubicle and woke her, weeping aloud with a crazed love that lasted until it was carried away without mercy by the violent wind of real life. Her name was Castorina and she was the queen of the house.

The cubicles in the hotel cost a peso for transient loves, but very few of us knew they cost the same for up to twenty-four hours. Castorina also introduced me to her shabby world, where the women invited poor clients to their gala breakfasts, lent them their soap, tended to their toothaches, and in cases of extreme urgency gave them charitable love.

But in the afternoons of my final old age no one remembered the immortal Castorina, dead for who knows how long, who had risen from the miserable corners of the river docks to the sacred throne of elder madam, wearing a pirate's patch over the eye she lost in a tavern brawl. Her last steady stud, a fortunate black from Camagüey called Jonás the Galley Slave, had been one of the great trumpet players in Havana until he lost his entire smile in a catastrophic train collision.

When I left that bitter visit I felt the shooting pain in my heart that I had not been able to relieve for three days using every kind of household concoction. The doctor I went to as an emergency patient was a member of an illustrious family, the grandson of the doctor who had seen me when I was forty-two, and it frightened me that he looked the same, for his premature baldness, glasses of a hopeless myopic, and inconsolable sadness made him as aged as his grandfather had been at seventy. He made a meticulous examination of my entire body with the concentration of a goldsmith. He listened to my chest and back and checked my blood pressure, the reflexes in my knee, the depths of my eyes, the color of my lower lids. During pauses, while I changed position on the examining table, he asked me questions so vague and rapid I almost did not have time to think of the answers. After an hour he looked at me with a happy smile. Well, he said, I don't think there's anything I can do for you. What do you mean? That your condition is the best it can be at your age. How curious, I said, your grandfather told me the same thing when I was forty-two, and it's as if no time has passed. You'll always find someone who'll tell you this, he said, because you'll always be some age. Trying to provoke him into a terrifying sentence, I said: The only definitive thing is death. Yes, he said, but it isn't easy to get there when one's condition is as good as yours. I'm really sorry I can't oblige you.

They were noble memories, but on the eve of August 29 I felt the immense weight of the century that lay ahead of me, impassive, as I climbed the stairs to my house with leaden steps. Then I saw my mother, Florina de Dios, in my bed, which had been hers until her death, and she gave me the same blessing she had given the last time I saw her, two hours before she died. In a state of emotional upheaval I understood this as the final warning, and I called Rosa Cabarcas to bring me my girl that very night, in the event that my hopes for surviving until the final breath of my ninetieth year went unfulfilled. I called her again at eight, and once again she repeated that it was not possible. It has to be, at any price, I shouted in terror. She hung up without saying goodbye, but fifteen minutes later she called back:

"All right, she's here."

I arrived at twenty past ten and handed Rosa Cabarcas the last letters of my life, with my arrangements for the girl after my terrible end. She thought I had been affected by the stabbing and said with a mocking air: If you're going to die don't do it here, just imagine. But I told her: Say I was run down by the Puerto Colombia train, that poor, pitiful piece of junk that couldn't kill anybody.

That night, prepared for everything, I lay down on my back to wait for my final pain in the first instant of my ninety-first birthday. I heard distant bells, I detected the fragrance of Delgadina's soul as she slept on her side, I heard a shout on the horizon, the sobs of someone who perhaps had died a century earlier in the room. Then I put out the light with my last breath, intertwined my fingers with hers so I could lead her by the hand, and counted the twelve strokes of midnight with my twelve final tears until the roosters began to crow, followed by the bells of glory, the fiesta fireworks that celebrated the jubilation of having survived my ninetieth year safe and sound.

My first words were for Rosa Cabarcas: I'll buy the house, everything, including the shop and the orchard. She said: Let's make an old people's bet, signed before a notary: whoever survives keeps everything that belongs to the other one. No, because if I die, everything has to be for her. It amounts to the same thing, said Rosa Cabarcas, I take care of the girl and then I leave her everything, what's yours and what's mine; I don't have anybody else in the world. In the meantime, we'll remodel your room and put in good plumbing, air-conditioning, and your books and music.

"Do you think she'll agree?"

"Ah, my sad scholar, it's all right for you to be old

but not an asshole," said Rosa Cabarcas, weak with laughter. "That poor creature's head over heels in love with you."

I went out to the street, radiant, and for the first time I could recognize myself on the remote horizon of my first century. My house, silent and in order at six-fifteen, began to enjoy the colors of a joyous dawn. Damiana was singing at the top of her voice in the kitchen, and the resuscitated cat twined his tail around my ankles and continued walking with me to my writing table. I was arranging my languishing papers, the inkwell, the goose quill, when the sun broke through the almond trees in the park and the river mail packet, a week late because of the drought, bellowed as it entered the canal in the port. It was, at last, real life, with my heart safe and condemned to die of happy love in the joyful agony of any day after my hundredth birthday.

May 2004

GABRIEL GARCÍA MÁRQUEZ

ONE HUNDRED YEARS OF SOLITUDE

'The greatest novel in any language of the last 50 years. Marquez writes in this lyrical, magical language that no-one else can do' Salman Rushdie

'Many years later, as he faced the firing squad, Colonel Aureliano Buendía was to remember that distant afternoon when his father took him to discover ice ...'

Pipes and kettledrums herald the arrival of gypsies on their annual visit to Macondo, the newly founded village where José Arcadio Buendía and his strong-willed wife, Úrsula, have started their new life. As the mysterious Melquíades excites Aureliano Buendía's father with new inventions and tales of adventure, neither can know the significance of the indecipherable manuscript that the old gypsy passes into their hands.

Through plagues of insomnia, civil war, hauntings and vendettas, the many tribulations of the Buendía household push memories of the manuscript aside. Few remember its existence and only one will discover the hidden message that it holds...

'Should be required reading for the entire human race' *New York Times*

'No lover of fiction can fail to respond to the grace of Márquez's writing' *Sunday Telegraph*

'It's the most magical book I have ever read. I think Márquez has influenced the world' Carolina Herrera

GABRIEL GARCÍA MÁRQUEZ

LOVE IN THE TIME OF CHOLERA

'An amazing celebration of the many kinds of love between men and women'
The Times

'*It was inevitable: the scent of bitter almonds always reminded him of the fate of unrequited love …*'

Fifty-one years, nine months and four days have passed since Fermina Daza rebuffed hopeless romantic Florentino Ariza's impassioned advances and married Dr. Juvenal Urbino instead. During that half century, Florentino has fallen into the arms of many delighted women, but has loved none but Fermina. Having sworn his eternal love to her, he lives for the day when he can court her again.

When Fermina's husband is killed trying to retrieve his pet parrot from a mango tree, Florentino seizes his chance to declare his enduring love. But can young love find new life in the twilight of their lives?

'A love story of astonishing power and delicious comedy' *Newsweek*

'A delight' Melvyn Bragg

GABRIEL GARCÍA MÁRQUEZ

THE STORY OF A SHIPWRECKED SAILOR

'A gripping tale of survival' *The Times*

'*On February 22 we were told that we would be returning to Columbia …*'

In 1955, eight crew members of *Caldas*, a Colombian destroyer, were swept overboard. Velasco alone survived, drifting on a raft for ten days without food or water. Márquez retells the survivor's amazing tale of endurance, from his loneliness and thirst to his determination to survive.

The Story of a Shipwrecked Sailor was Márquez's first major, and controversial, work, published in a Colombian newspaper, *El Espectador*, in 1955 and then in book form in 1970.

'The story of Velasco on his raft, his battle with sharks over a succulent fish, his hallucinations, his capture of a seagull which he was unable to eat, his subsequent droll rescue, has all the grip of archetypal myth. Reads like an epic' *Independent*

GABRIEL GARCÍA MÁRQUEZ

CHRONICLE OF A DEATH FORETOLD

'My favourite book by one of the world's greatest authors. You're in the hands of a master' Mariella Frostrup

'On the day they were going to kill him, Santiago Nasar got up at five-thirty in the morning to wait for the boat the bishop was coming on …'

When newly-wed Angela Vicario and Bayardo San Román are left to their wedding night, Bayardo discovers that his new wife is no virgin. Disgusted, he returns Angela to her family home that very night, where her humiliated mother beats her savagely and her two brothers demand to know her violator, whom she names as Santiago Nasar.

As he wakes to thoughts of the previous night's revelry, Santiago is unaware of the slurs that have been cast against him. But with Angela's brothers set on avenging their family honour, soon the whole town knows who they plan to kill, where, when and why.

'A masterpiece' *Evening Standard*

'A work of high explosiveness – the proper stuff of Nobel prizes. An exceptional novel' *The Times*

'Brilliant writer, brilliant book' *Guardian*

GABRIEL GARCÍA MÁRQUEZ

IN EVIL HOUR

'A masterly book' *Guardian*

'César Montero was dreaming about elephants. He'd seen them at the movies on Sunday ...'

Only moments later, César is led away by police as they clear the crowds away from the man he has just killed.

But César is not the only man to be riled by the rumours being spread in his Colombian hometown – under the cover of darkness, someone creeps through the streets sticking malicious posters to walls and doors. Each night the respectable townsfolk retire to their beds fearful that they will be the subject of the following morning's lampoons.

As paranoia seeps through the town and the delicate veil of tranquility begins to slip, can the perpetrator be uncovered before accusation and violence leave the inhabitants' sanity in tatters?

'*In Evil Hour* was the book which was to inspire my own career as a novelist. I owe my writing voice to that one book!' Jim Crace

'Belongs to the very best of Márquez's work ... Should on no account be missed' *Financial Times*

'A splendid achievement' *The Times*

GABRIEL GARCÍA MÁRQUEZ

OF LOVE AND OTHER DEMONS

'Superb and intensely readable' *Time Out*

'An ash-gray dog with a white blaze on its forehead burst onto the rough terrain of the market on the first Sunday of December ...'

When a witch doctor appears on the doorstep of the Marquis de Casalduero prophesizing a plague of rabies in their Colombian seaport, he dismisses her claims – until, that is, he hears that his young daughter, Sierva María, was one of four people bitten by a rabid dog, and the only one to survive.

Sierva María appears completely unscathed – but as rumours of the plague spread, the Marquis and his wife wonder at her continuing good health. In a town consumed by superstition, it's not long before they, and everyone else, put her survival down to a demonic possession and begin to see her supernatural powers as the cause of the town's woes. Only the young priest charged with exorcising the evil spirit recognizes the girl's sanity, but can he convince the town that it's not her that needs healing?

'Brilliantly moving. A tour de force' A.S. Byatt

'A compassionate, witty and unforgettable masterpiece' *Daily Telegraph*

'At once nostalgic and satiric, a resplendent fable' *Sunday Times*

He just wanted a decent book to read ...

Not too much to ask, is it? It was in 1935 when Allen Lane, Managing Director of Bodley Head Publishers, stood on a platform at Exeter railway station looking for something good to read on his journey back to London. His choice was limited to popular magazines and poor-quality paperbacks – the same choice faced every day by the vast majority of readers, few of whom could afford hardbacks. Lane's disappointment and subsequent anger at the range of books generally available led him to found a company – and change the world.

'We believed in the existence in this country of a vast reading public for intelligent books at a low price, and staked everything on it'
Sir Allen Lane, 1902–1970, founder of Penguin Books

The quality paperback had arrived – and not just in bookshops. Lane was adamant that his Penguins should appear in chain stores and tobacconists, and should cost no more than a packet of cigarettes.

Reading habits (and cigarette prices) have changed since 1935, but Penguin still believes in publishing the best books for everybody to enjoy. We still believe that good design costs no more than bad design, and we still believe that quality books published passionately and responsibly make the world a better place.

So wherever you see the little bird – whether it's on a piece of prize-winning literary fiction or a celebrity autobiography, political tour de force or historical masterpiece, a serial-killer thriller, reference book, world classic or a piece of pure escapism – you can bet that it represents the very best that the genre has to offer.

Whatever you like to read – trust Penguin.